massive

*Also by Julia Bell*

HARD SHOULDER
(co-edited with Jackie Gay)

ENGLAND CALLING
(co-edited with Jackie Gay)

CREATIVE WRITING COURSEBOOK
(co-edited with Paul Magrs)

JULIA BELL

# massive

YOUNG PICADOR

First published 2002 by Young Picador
An imprint of Pan Macmillan Ltd
Pan Macmillan, 20 New Wharf Road, London N1 9RR
Basingstoke and Oxford
Associated companies throughout the world
www.panmacmillan.com

ISBN 0 330 41547 6

1 3 5 7 9 8 6 4 2

A CIP catalogue record for this book is available from
the British Library

Phototypeset by Intype London Ltd
Printed and bound in Great Britain by Mackays of Chatham plc, Kent

Nuff respect to the friends and family massive –


The Bell family, Rachel Bradford, Maggie Braley,
Lesa Carniegie, Louise D'Arcens, Bex Farley,
Jackie Gay, Ness Harbar, Emma Hargrave,
Mo Herdman, Laura Hird, Tina Jackson, JpJ,
Paschal Kane, Penny & Dave Rendall, Michèle Roberts,
Jerry Sheldon, Ali Smith, Barbara Watts and
Sara Wingate Gray.

And a big up to the Tindal Street Fiction Group, my
editor Sarah Davies, and my patient and encouraging
agent, Annette Green.

'...it is certain that I am really distinct from my body, and can exist without it.'

*Descartes*

*For all the girlfriends*

# 1

'If I was as big as her I'd kill myself,' Mum says, pointing at a picture of Marilyn Monroe in her magazine.

I'm sitting at the kitchen table waiting for my toast to brown. If I don't watch it, it will burn. Mum always buys lo-salt Danish bread that toasts really quickly, the kind that has more air in it than flour. On her new diet she's allowed two slices at breakfast, along with 30g of Special K with skimmed milk.

'You'd tell me, wouldn't you? If I got that big?'

I look at her, I can see her bones through her clothes.

'Of course,' I lie.

She watches me as I spread Gold Ultra Lite on my toast.

'Don't use so much, Carmen.'

My name is Carmen because Mum likes to imagine that she's got Spanish blood in her. That and the fact that I bawled my eyes out, 'like some bloody opera singer,' for six months after I was born.

'You're unlucky,' she says to me sometimes, looking me up and down, assessing my already plump chest, my thick hips, my freckles. 'You'll end up with a Mediterranean figure, like your nan. You'll always have to watch your weight.'

At fourteen I already know this much about my own destiny. If she wanted me to be tall and skinny she should have given me a different name.

Mum has been on a diet ever since I can remember. She has more diet books than the town library. A whole shelf of them above the cooker. Diets for hips and thighs, for chests, for rapid weight loss, for toning, for shaping. Books by celebrities, doctors, sports stars, cranks. Diets that tell you to eat nothing but grapefruit, yogurt, skimmed milk, milkshakes, fish, cabbages, broad beans.

*Don't snack!* They all say that. *Don't snack!* Don't fill your mouth in between meals, chew gum, drink water, nibble carrots. No crisps, no chocolate, no cola, no chips, no calories.

Mum likes to think we do the same diets together. She loses but I stay the same, or sometimes I put on a few pounds. She can't understand it, she says I must be cursed with a slow metabolism. What she doesn't acknowledge is that I don't stick to them properly. That I eat fries and Big Macs. That I snack.

On the fridge there are lists of foods and weights and portions that change every day.

This week it's a *Power Diet!™*. *The Power is You!*

Today it says:

**Breakfast**
*One half grapefruit/30g Special K*
*Toast x 2*
*Spread ¹⁄₂ teaspoon*

**Lunch**

*Consommé*

*Carrots 225g (washed)*

**Supper**

*Power Shake™ (Vanilla)*

**Snacks**

*Dried-fruit mix (50g)*

These lists are stuck on with novelty magnets that have slogans like: *Don't Do It! A Moment on Your Lips, Forever on Your Hips!* She gets them mail order from a place in America.

*The Power Diet™* comes complete with a month's supply of *Power Shakes™*, a handbook and a box of recipe cards for lo-cal meals, most of them involving carrots and brown rice.

According to the box, NASA developed *Power Shakes™* as meal replacements for astronauts. Inside the foil pouches is a thick, gloopy liquid, rich in vitamins and essential minerals, which you are supposed to dilute with water. Mum let me try one when the box arrived, DHL from California. Unlike the picture of a thick, frothing shake, it was thin and watery and had a weird, metallic aftertaste. You're only supposed to have three a week as replacements; Mum has them for nearly every main meal.

She shuts her magazine and opens the *Power Diet™* handbook. It is full of Positive Affirmations, slogans to make you 'think and feel in a more powerful way'.

*'You are a beautiful person.'* She smiles. 'There. Doesn't that make you feel better?'

3

Dad comes in looking tired, his clothes crumpled. Looks like he spent the night in the garage again.

'Slept with your computers, did you?' Mum says, raising an eyebrow at him. He's set up a workshop in the garage, because Mum won't let him bring his stuff into the house. 'I can't deal with the mess, Brian. All those itty bitty bits of wire get stuck in the carpet and ruin my tights.'

He grunts and opens the fridge. 'Who's for fried eggs?'

'Yes, please,' I say.

'Brian,' Mum doesn't look up. 'We're supposed to be on a *diet*. How is she ever going to learn if you keep giving her food?'

He doesn't say anything and lights the flame on the gas.

Dad ignores Mum's diets, mutters about them being whacko, nuts, that they only end up making her sick. 'They don't make you look any better, Maria.'

She moans about this, says it's not fair that she still has to buy his full-fat food while she's dieting. There are three separate shelves in the fridge. At the top, Mum's tubs: Tupperware full of carrot sticks and celery, boiled rice, slices of chicken with the skin removed, lemon wedges, grapefruit halves, cottage cheese, no-fat yogurt. My shelf is supposed to be in the middle but Dad always mixes things up. He puts his leftover takeaway trays back on my shelf next to all the Weight Watchers ready meals and lo-fat spreads. Mum ignores these little digs, muttering under her breath as she puts the butter back on the bottom shelf that he doesn't understand a thing about feeding a family.

He takes a box of extra-large free-range eggs from his shelf and asks me if I want my egg sunny side up, over easy or upside down.

'Over easy, partner,' I say. It's our little joke; we like to pretend we're American.

'Do you have to *fry* them? I don't know how you can eat them like that, all that *mucus.*' Dad cracks two eggs in his fist over the pan. The slimy insides drop into the hot fat and start spitting. 'Brian, it's making me *nauseous.*' He doesn't say anything, just carries on shifting the pan around over the flame.

When he puts my egg in front of me, the yolk all runny and soaking into my toast, she makes exaggerated puking noises. I turn away from her and eat it really quickly.

'Fried egg on toast, 300 calories. At least. You'll be on lettuce all week now, you know, Carmen,' she says. 'After all that fat.'

Later, she complains that she can smell it on her clothes. 'I stink like a chip shop,' she says, giving herself an extra squirt of perfume. 'It's disgusting.'

My mother works in a clothes shop in town. Waltons for Women. An exclusive boutique where they sell clothes that cost more than most people's wages. Top designer labels like Gucci, Prada, Versace, Armani, Paul Smith. Mum got the job part-time when she was convalescing, switching to full-time last year.

Mrs Walton who owns the shop is delighted, she says Mum has a real flair for the London fashions. Profits are up twenty-five per cent in the two years since Mum's been working there. She even lets Mum do some of the buying now. This week she's got appointments in Birmingham and Leeds.

'The only way is up, baby,' she says, zipping up her Louis Vuitton overnight case and patting herself on the thigh.

She's away in Birmingham and I will have a Big Mac for tea if Dad's 'cooking', from the new McDonald's they built on the edge of the valley.

I am at home watching TV, eating a Movie Bag of tortilla chips bought on the way home from school, waiting for Dad to get back from work. The pretty blonde girl in the Australian soap kisses her new lover. I feel a pang. I've never had a boyfriend, not like Janice who's nearly gone all the way already.

My fingers have turned a violent orange from the cheese powder. I wipe them on my Adidas trackpants, making greasy tiger stripes across my thighs. The bag is already empty; my mouth is shrivelling from all the salt. I wonder what else there is in the house to eat. If only I didn't feel so hungry all the time.

He should be home by now. But he's probably forgotten that he's supposed to be looking after me tonight. I eat the box of snack fruit that Mum left in the cupboard: 350g, a week's worth of dried sultanas and raisins.

Dad owns half of a computer business – NorTech – a name Mum says sounds like someone trying to bring up phlegm. He builds the computers from scratch to the customer's specifications, and his business partner, Moira, runs the shop in town, taking all the orders and selling peripherals like printers and software and Mickey Mouse mats and glow-in-the dark joysticks. Dad says that in the past few years, with the technological revolution and everything, business has never been so good.

Moira has a bigger house over in the next valley. Her husband John put money into the business when it started, and they have two sons, Adrian and Sam, who both go to private schools. Adrian, the eldest, is the same age as me.

When Mum got sick, Dad used to take me over there for sleepovers. Moira made proper teas, giant dishes of macaroni cheese, lasagne, shepherd's pie. 'Your dad has been under such a lot of *strain*,' she said to me in her creamy voice, scooping a small mountain of pasta on to my plate. 'Looking after you is the *least* I can do.'

When Mum came back from hospital she banned me from going there. She said that Moira was nosy, interfering. 'Everything's been getting far too *cosy* while I've been away.'

I watch the news, a holiday programme and half of another soap before I hear his key in the door.

'Hiya kid,' is the first thing he says as he flops into the sofa next to me. He has McDonald's bags in his hands.

'Did you get me a Big Mac?' I ask.

'Don't tell your mother,' he says, winking.

My mother left a whole fridge of instructions and portions for me. Today's affirmation is: *Don't put it off! Do it Now!*

I'm supposed to be eating a lo-fat ready-made cheese and ham tagliatelle. A Weight Watchers special, under 400 calories and less than one per cent fat. Instead, I'm letting the grease of a Big Mac slide down my chin. Dad doesn't look at me as he chews on his Fillet O' Fish. He plugs in the PlayStation, while he holds the burger in his mouth. He sits down, cross-legged in front of it like one of those brass Buddha statues they sell in Margy's Mystic Shop in town. He plays *Wipeout*. Always *Wipeout* or *Colin McRae Rally*. He likes fast driving games. The kind that move through landscapes at hundreds of miles an hour. He's better at it than me. But only because he never lets me have a go.

He's not my real dad, but Mum's been with him since I was three and I can't remember much before then, so I guess he is really, nearly, my dad. Mum won't let me talk about it. 'Brian's your father and that's an end to it. You don't want to know about before. I'll tell you when you're twenty-one.'

He scrunches up the greasy wrappers. 'Make us a cuppa, love,' he says.

'Did you get me any sweets?' I ask.

He reaches in his pocket and gives me a Mars Bar. It's warm where it's been close to his skin and when I open it, the chocolate has melted and stuck to the wrapper.

When I was younger, before Mum got sick, she used to dress me up and take me places. Ballet classes, acting classes, singing classes. The pictures of me that she keeps round the house are all of then, when I was nine and ten, Mummy's little fairy princess, with tiara, wings and sparkly tights.

Dad said it was her diets made her sick, but Mum says that she was depressed.

When she went to hospital Dad let me buy my own clothes. These days I'm into sportswear, trainers, track-pants, hooded tops. Now Mum's better she moans about it.

'You've got all the things I never had,' she says to me. 'And you have to dress like a *hairdresser*. I thought girls wanted to be sophisticated these days.' She tries to get me to buy the kind of things she would wear but every-thing she buys is the wrong size, the wrong shape, the wrong cut. 'I think it's time you started wearing a bra,' she said, when I couldn't get into the size ten T-shirt she bought me from Top Shop. 'You should have *told* me.'

She bought me a girlie purple one, but I don't wear it. I don't want to have tits.

In the morning he gives me a lift to school in his car. It's a yellow sports convertible with shiny wheels and black leather seats. He got it last year as a bonus. Mum just snorted when she saw it. 'It's the colour of a banana, Brian.'

I ask him if he thinks Mum will get sick again.

He sighs. 'If your mother says she's better I'm not going to contradict her.'

She was in hospital for months. Dad said it was because she was throwing up her food instead of swallowing it, that she was crafty, untrustworthy. When she came out, Dad made her promise to eat properly, 'for Carmen's sake, if not for mine'.

As we pull up outside the gates I look to see if any of the town girls are watching. Everyone round here thinks my dad is a bit of a nerd, they call him Boffin, and Gateshead, because he looks like Bill Gates.

Even Janice calls him Gateshead. 'Oh, come on, Carmen,' she said, when I complained that she was being rude about my family. 'So what if he's a nerd? No one else knows how to fix computers like him.'

'Here.' He gives me a KitKat. 'Sweets for my sweet.' He kisses me on the forehead.

His aftershave makes me sneeze.

'Sneeze three times, you'll get a letter,' he says, his eyes scrunching up behind his glasses.

'You what?'

'Nothing, just something my mum used to say. Maybe

it was a wish. Sneeze three times, you can make a wish.'
He winks at me. 'See you later, kiddo.'

As his car pulls away into the traffic, I think about
Mum, away on her business trip. Don't let her get sick,
I wish.

My best friend, Janice Ramsden, has just started going
out with a boy in the sixth form and I've spent all morning
listening to her swooning about him and hanging around
waiting for her to finish kissing him during break.

Lunchtime, I'm on my own because they've gone down
town for the afternoon to snog in the park instead. She
says she's going to do it with him soon; she's just waiting
for his parents to go on holiday so they can use the double
bed. I'm listening to the All Saints on my Walkman,
eating sausage and chips, staring into space, not thinking.
Mum would probably stop my dinner money if she knew.
I'm supposed to buy salads and mineral water, a couple
of apples and pears.

I know she's back before I see her suitcase in the hall. I
can smell her perfume, Chanel No 5, in the hallway. She's
lying on the couch with a big black folder on her knees.
She's doing sums with a calculator. When she sees me
she snaps the folder shut.

'Hello, darling,' she says. 'How was school?'

'You're not supposed to be back till Friday,' I say.

She wrinkles her nose. 'You stink of chocolate.' I back
away from her.

'Janice got some.'

'And you didn't buy any?'

I shake my head, but I can tell she doesn't believe me.

Dad buys chicken pie and chips for his tea. He doesn't even bother with a plate, eating it in front of us straight out of the paper.

'Brian, please. We're eating.'

I stir my Weight Watchers ratatouille that tastes too strongly of tinned tomatoes.

'Is that what you call it?' Dad mutters.

He hasn't even finished his chips when he bundles the papers into a ball and pushes them in the bin. 'I've got work to do,' he says, picking up his briefcase.

'Mind you remember it's still your turn to take Carmen to school in the morning.' But the back door into the garage has already slammed. 'That's the last we'll see of *him*, tonight,' she says, biting her lip.

I go to my room and unpack my homework. Put the radio on my Walkman and flick through a magazine. I don't hear her coming in so that when she puts her hand on my shoulder, I nearly jump out of my skin.

'Doesn't look like homework to me,' she says, pointing at my magazine as I fumble to get the earphones out of my ears.

She sits on my bed and lights a cigarette. She's bored, I can tell. She wants to talk about her trip.

'I saw your nan,' she says, 'when I was in Birmingham.'

I was born in Birmingham; it's where Mum comes from. Usually she talks about it like it's a black hole, full of roads and factories. She told me once that when Queen Victoria went through it on the train she drew the curtains in her carriage so she didn't have to see the view.

'How come you didn't stay, then? I thought you were supposed to come back on *Friday*.'

'Well,' – she pauses to drag on her cigarette – 'that's

because I've got some *news* for you.' She says 'news' really slowly, blowing out smoke as she speaks.

'What?'

'How would you feel if we were to move away from here, one day?'

'Move where?' Something's going on. 'Why?'

She looks at her nails. 'Well there's a possibility, just a *tiny* possibility that I might get a job in Birmingham.'

'Would Dad come with us?'

'I haven't discussed it with him yet. I wanted to talk to you first.'

I shrug. 'Sounds OK,' I say. 'If Dad comes with us.'

She smashes her cigarette into the ashtray. 'We don't need him, sweetheart,' she says, quietly. 'Not any more.'

When she's gone, I suck on the King Size Snickers that Dad gave me earlier. He slipped it in my schoolbag when she wasn't looking. I lick the chocolate off all the peanuts and crunch them slowly, one by one. I don't reckon we'll go to Birmingham. Mum's always full of mad schemes. Last year it was a holiday in the Caribbean. Dad even booked the tickets and everything. Then, suddenly, two weeks before, she got scared she was going to get a blood clot on the plane. She ripped up her passport and left it in bits in the kitchen.

When I've finished the Snickers, I post the wrapper down the gap between my headboard and the mattress. That's the trouble with snacking, it makes you sneaky.

Moira tells Mum that it's just a social visit. She brings some home-made shortbread, wrapped up in greaseproof paper, and Adrian, still in his sludgy-green school uniform.

12

Mum tries to look delighted, but I can tell from the shadow that passes across her eyes that she is terrified.

She keeps Moira on the doorstep. 'Oh, you'll have to excuse me, the house is a *complete* tip. I was just cleaning up.'

Moira is the kind of woman who sweeps into a room; who wears velvet wraps, long, expensive skirts, woollen winter coats; who doesn't take no for an answer. She sells loads of computers, especially to the kinds of women who want to seem as modern and 'on the button' as Moira is herself. Dad calls her his secret weapon.

'I just wanted to see how you were getting along. Brian said you were much better.' She smiles understandingly, taking a step closer towards the door. 'It must have been so difficult for you.'

Adrian stands behind her, drawing circles in the gravel with his trainers. He's got throbbing yellow zits on his forehead. I hide behind Mum and make faces at him.

Mum holds firm, even though Moira seems to tower over her. 'I'm terribly sorry,' she says, 'I'm in the middle of cleaning.' And she starts to shut the door.

When Moira has gone, Mum gets upset. She says it's just another tactic of Dad's, that he's spying on her. She throws the shortbread away without unwrapping it.

'I know I'm not confident like them,' she says, screwing up her face. 'I know that I'm a *fraud*.'


'I'm back on form,' she gasps, running into the house and bouncing a little on her feet. 'I'm back on top.'

It's early summer and school is just about to break up. *The Power Diet!*™ is working. Mum says she's never felt so powerful in her life.

She's sweating, her face flushed. She drinks a glass of

water and takes a few deep breaths. 'Oh, that hill,' she says. 'It's a killer.' She smiles at me. 'You should come with me, do you good. Get a few pounds off you.'

She puts Danny Rampling on the stereo and gets her cleaning things out. All the products she buys look like medicines, they all say *With Bleach* or *Antibacterial*. 'Come on, Carmen,' she says, shifting me off my seat. 'Go and get changed and put your uniform in the wash. I want to clean this place up. It's unhygienic.'

I sit in the lounge, do a few laps on *Wipeout*, get bored with it and switch to *Colin McRae Rally* instead. House music *tsk-tsks* under the drone of the Hoover.

'I've got a bone to pick with you.' Her voice, too close, makes me jump. She switches off the PlayStation with her foot. 'I found all this,' she holds up a Morrison's bag, 'under your bed.'

She tips up the bag; wrappers skitter across the floor in a cascade of shimmering colours. Foil from KitKats, scrunched up Mars Bar wrappers, Snickers wrappers, empty Chocolate Button packets, Quality Street papers from Christmas, crisp packets folded into knob helmets like the boys at school make to flick at people, the purple Dairy Milk foil, the gold from Galaxy, a whole handful of greaseproof wrappers from penny chews, Crunchie, Twix Ice Cream, Toffee Crisp, Flake, M&M's, Fudge, even a Mars Easter-egg box that I folded up so it would go through the gap.

I don't know where to look. 'Dad gave me them,' I say.

'Your bloody father.' She blows air between her teeth, making a hissing noise. 'Just because he gives them to you doesn't mean you *have* to eat them. No wonder you

14

aren't losing anything. Dear God, girl, do you *want* to be fat and unhappy?'

'I'm not unhappy.'

'Put your shoulders back then.'

'But my room is *private*.' My voice is starting to wobble. It comes out all pathetic and high-pitched; I stare into the snowstorm on the TV screen.

'Not until you pay your own rent it's not.' She throws the plastic bag at me. 'Pick them up,' she says. 'It's disgusting.' She stalks out of the room. I gather the wrappers and stuff them back in the plastic bag. Some of them are really dusty. I can feel tears welling up behind my eyes, but I bite my lip. Don't cry, I think, don't cry.

# 2

I was only two and a half when Mum moved away from Birmingham to be with Brian. Sometimes I think I can remember what it was like. If I close my eyes and think really hard, I see a yellow kitchen on a sunny day, powder-puff clouds in the sky, blue-checked curtains furling like flags in the breeze.

Mum has pictures that she keeps under the bed, of me in fat nappies, crawling around the garden in a place called Hall Green. She showed me Birmingham on the map once, a knot of buildings and roads, bang in the middle of the country.

She never usually talks about it. She doesn't even keep any photographs of the family round the house, and we never go there to visit. These last few weeks she's been full of it.

'Things have really changed in the last ten years, *everyone* says so.'

She shows me some glossy brochure advertising all the new redevelopment. 'The city's going really upmarket,' she says, 'like they did to Leeds.'

She says she's going to take me there in the summer holidays for a trial period. Dad's not coming with us because Mum says he's too busy, 'and anyway, he's not invited. This is about me, sweetheart. For once in my life

I'm going to put myself first. You'll love it,' she says, 'I know you will. More stuff to do than round here. And there's all the family. Your nana and grandad. It'll be exciting for you. Whole new world.' She does a little shimmy when she says this, clapping her hands above her head and clicking her fingers like she's in a pop video or something.

Although Mum doesn't talk about her, she's also got an older sister in Birmingham – Lisa. She's a beautician. Every Christmas she sends us a gift set of Body Shop bubble baths.

'Cheap gestures,' my mother said when she opened this year's pink-themed basket. 'A few smellies doesn't make up for much.'

My mother and Lisa don't really talk any more. 'You haven't got a sister, so you wouldn't understand,' she said when I asked why. 'Always the *poseur* my sister. Fancied herself as a bit of a pop star, she did. Thought she was going to get into the big time but after all her posing around she ended up doing nails. There's a lesson for you, Carmen. Don't get ideas above your station, you'll just end up doing nails when you're forty.' She laughed when she said this, the noise catching in her throat, making her sound like she was choking.

'Look,' she says, putting her arms around my shoulders, 'I know I haven't been around for you as much as I should recently, but all that's going to change, promise you. How about we try again?'

She looks me in the face. I can see where her make-up is bleeding into the lines under her eyes. 'Yeah?'

I nod and she presses her lips against my forehead. They are dry and scratchy.

17

'I thought maybe this one.' She points at her magazine. Liz Taylor's Classic Diet Tips.

'But she's dying,' I say.

'We're all doing that, darling. But she looked good in the fifties, didn't she?' Mum says, pointing at a picture of a pouting Liz Taylor. She sighs. 'It's a diet for the fuller figure, you know, a little at a time, so's you don't get cravings.'

My bedroom smells of Pledge and Odour Eaters; she's even folded all my sweatshirts into neat piles in the ward-robe. I sit with my back to the door and peel open a Chocolate Orange bar, sucking on the segment-shaped pieces. I don't like all this talk of Birmingham. There's something funny going on. Something they're not telling me.

When Dad comes back I go downstairs to talk to him, chewing sugarfree gum in case Mum smells the chocolate.

But they're already arguing. Dad says that if she goes to Birmingham, 'It's the end of the road for us, Maria.'

I hover in the corridor, not wanting to go in.

Mum changes the subject, mutters something rude about Moira.

'This isn't about her. You're *obsessed*,' Dad says. 'She's done nothing wrong. Poor woman's terrified of you.'

'Well, *is* she going to America with you?'

'Yes. She owns half the company, Maria. There's nothing funny going on. It's you,' he says, 'and your bloody diets. That's the only funny thing going on around here. Thing is, it's not funny, it's *tragic*.'

'This hasn't got anything to do with food, Brian. I want my life back. I want *prospects*. I'm not spending the rest

18

of my life up here while you swan around with Moira. And anyway, if you had any loyalty *I* would have her job.'

'You were sick, Maria.'

'I'm not now though, am I? I could sell computers if I wanted to.'

Dad laughs at this. 'You don't even know how to switch one on, Maria.'

'See what I mean? You don't think I can do anything, do you? Well screw you.' She screams this last bit at him. '*Screw* you.'

Janice's new boyfriend is off sick so she's hanging out with me again.

'Give us a chip.'

It's lunchtime and she's watching me eat a plateful of sausage and chips.

'You done it yet then?' I say, though I don't really have to ask. I can tell from the way she walks that she has learned something, a secret that she can't share with anyone.

She won't meet my eye. 'Sort of,' she says. 'I never let him put it in. I don't want to get pregnant.' She pauses. 'At least, not until after I've finished school.'

'Don't you want to go to college?'

She turns up her nose. 'And pay all that money? My brother's doing that, and he'll be loads in debt when he's finished. Anyway, Karl says he'll support me.' She steals another handful of chips off my plate. 'We're gonna get a flat together.'

She shows me the mobile phone that he bought her. I feel a stab of jealousy. 'I'm going to go to college first, before I move in with anybody,' I say defiantly. I know this will piss her off because she's pretty crap at school.

19

She always gets the worst marks unless she copies from me.

She changes the subject. 'What you doing over the holidays?'

'Going to Birmingham,' I say, dipping my last chip in a puddle of sauce.

She laughs, 'Bummer. That's so, like, *unfair*. Bring us back a stick of rock.'


The woman is looking at herself in the shop mirror. 'I'm not sure,' she says, 'at my age you have to worry about necklines.'

Mum fusses in the background, tweaking imaginary bits of fluff from the shoulders of the dress.

'And see-through, I don't want it to be see-through.'

'Oh, but we have a very *good* alterations service, Mrs Feathers. We can so easily sew in a flesh undergarment.'

Mum smiles at Mrs Feathers as if she is the most beautiful creature she has ever seen. This is a tactic Mum says works every time.

Oh, go on then,' Mrs Feathers says, her cheeks gently blushing. 'I really shouldn't but Henry *did* tell me to treat myself.'

I am sitting behind the counter, crunching cola cubes. Mum gives me a funny look. 'Who gave you money for sweets? Don't make such a noise. It puts people off.'

We're supposed to be going to Morrison's to get the shopping in, but we're late because Mum has been helping Mrs Feathers with her dress. Mum is dedicated to her customers. Something which has made her popular with Mrs Walton.

'I know how to tell people the things they want to hear,'

she says afterwards, standing outside the shop smoking a cigarette. 'I know how easy it is to be deluded.'

We wheel our trolley through the sliding glass doors. Mum picks up a special-offer leaflet and looks at it. Two chickens for the price of one. 'That ought to sort your father out.'

I jump up on the trolley with one foot and ride it like a scooter, aiming for the banks of bananas.

'Carmen! Stop messing.' Mum runs after me, grabbing the handle of the trolley.

We spend ages in Produce, fingering the fruit and veg. Mum isn't happy until she's pinched and poked and prodded and squeezed most of the things on display.

She picks up an orange and shows it to me. 'See the skin?' she says, 'that's what will happen to your thighs when you get old and fat. Think of that next time you eat a cake.' She picks up an avocado and puts it in her trolley, then a few seconds later retraces her steps and puts it back. 'It's too hard,' she pronounces. 'Feel it, Carmen, it's like a stone. You can't eat that. Besides d'you know how many calories there are in those things? Millions. Might as well be eating blobs of lard.'

After Produce is the Bakery: long stainless-steel racks of hot bread, still steaming inside their cellophane. The buttery smell seems to seep into the whole of the shop. Mum picks up a big pillow of a loaf and holds it to my face, the plastic scratching my nose, 'Smell it,' she says, 'it's like drugs.'

She's quiet for a moment, and then she sighs and puts the bread back on the shelf.

After that, she's quicker. Grabbing boxes of Ryvita, pots of no-fat cottage cheese, tubs of lite yogurt, a selection of Weight Watchers frozen dinners. She lingers over the peanut butter in the Condiments aisle. For one joyful moment I think she might be about to put it in the trolley, but she reads the back and tuts.

'Devil's own food,' she says, putting it back on the shelf.

When we get to Poultry, Mum bends over the chiller cabinet and prods the chickens.

'Two for the price of one, Carmen, can't afford to pass that up,' she says, as if she is trying to explain herself to me. 'That'll stop your dad from moaning that I never buy any food. If it wasn't for him we wouldn't even be here.'

I wander up the aisle a bit and look at the ducks; the thick, yellowy fat and dark meat, strange next to the pallor of the chickens.

She follows me, pushing the trolley so it nudges into my thigh. 'What you looking at? Urgh,' she pokes a nail into the duck, 'it's all yellow.'

'It's supposed to be,' I say pointing at the label. 'It's free-range.'

At the checkout she gives me a pile of things to take back. A pack of iced buns, some frozen chips and a tub of double chocolate ice cream. I try to find interesting places to put them, deciding in the end that the ice cream should go on the shelf with the KitKats, the iced buns in the freezer next to the arctic rolls and the chips in among the bags of potatoes by the door.

'What you looking so pleased with yourself for?' Mum says when I come back to help her pack the bags.

Mum doesn't really like touching meat too much before it's cooked. A quick dash of salt, a crunch of pepper and a brush of Crisp & Dry before she bangs the door shut and spends ten minutes at the sink scrubbing her hands clean with antibacterial soap.

'You never know what's been growing on dead meat, you should always wash your hands after cooking, Carmen.'

I grunt at her from the kitchen table. I'm reading my magazine, trying not to think about how the chicken will come out, dry and stringy, the fat burned to a shell so it will lift off more easily.

When she's finished scrubbing, she sits down next to me and holds my hand. Her skin is rough and peeling. Her fingers are thin and light, like polystyrene.

'What's in the magazine? Is there a quiz? Let's do the quiz.'

I flick through it. *'Are You a Good Mate?'*

'Go on then, ask me.'

*'You're wearing a gorgeous new outfit. But when you get to the party you realize you mate is wearing the exact same thing. Do you: A. Go home and get changed? B. Laugh about it, and pretend to be sisters all night? C. Tell her to go and get changed, because, let's face it, you look better in it than she does?'*

I look at her. She's looking away into space, the smoke from her cigarette curling around her head.

*'Mum.* A, B or C?'

'Read me the question again.'

I sigh, and read her the question again.

She laughs this time. 'Oh C, definitely. Next.'

*'You both fancy the same bit of boy totty, he comes over to talk to you. Do you: A. Call your mate over to talk to him, too? B. Tell him about her? C. Grab your chance while it's yours?'*

'Too personal. Next.'

23

'Mu-*um*, you've got to answer all of them, or it won't work.'

'All right then, C again. What does it say if you're all Cs? I know I'm going to be all Cs. Does that mean I'm a bitch?'

She tries to snatch the magazine away from me.

'*Mum.*' I move away from her so she can't get it. '*Your mate has made a big fashion mistake and her outfit is a mess. Do you: A. Tell her before you go out and let her borrow an outfit from you? B. Tell her when you're out? C. Laugh about it behind her back?*'

'C again. Told you. Just read me what it says about C.'

'*You are a wicked mate. When it comes to scams and double crosses, you rule. You like to put yourself first and you don't care who knows it. But it might be a good idea to turn your evil powers to good use helping your mates. You have been warned.*'

Mum laughs. 'There. Told you so. A bitch.'

When the birds are cooked Mum pulls them out of the oven and puts them, still sizzling in their pans, on the table. She hacks off some big, thick pieces for me and puts them on my plate.

'That enough for you?' It looks like far too much. 'Have a bit more, I've done no vegetables or anything.' She adds a thigh to the pile.

She looks at the clock. 'I only did this for your father and he isn't even here. I just want to get away from all this' – she flaps her hands at the chicken – 'food. Know what I mean?'

She picks the thinnest slivers of meat and lays them on her plate in a dainty fan.

The meat is tasteless and chewy. Sinews get stuck

24

between my teeth. Mum cuts her piece into squares, and pushes it around her plate, tantalizing herself with it. I watch, holding my breath to see if she'll eat any. She prongs a bit, no bigger than a stamp, and lifts the fork to her mouth. She hesitates for what seems like ages, her hand trembling in front of her lips. Then, taking a breath, she closes her eyes and pushes the fork between her lips.

'It's a bit dry,' she says, chewing and swallowing, making a face as it goes down. It's so small, I wonder that she can feel it at all. She eats a few more squares and then pushes her plate aside. 'It'll be all right in sandwiches.'

'I'm going to pay you more attention from now on,' she says. 'I've been neglecting you.'

She sits really close to me on the sofa while I'm trying to get to the end of the lap on *Wipeout*. She distracts me and I crash into the side of a tunnel.

'I bought you some clothes for going away.'

In three separate bags there's a pink T-shirt with a heart on it, black Lycra trousers and a denim jacket, all from Top Shop in Manchester.

'I got you these as well, I hope they're going to fit you.' She hands me a Schuh bag. Inside is a pair of chunky, stack-heeled sandals.

My heart sinks as I look at the bags. It's all really slaggy stuff. More Janice's kind of thing than mine.

'Well, aren't you going to try it all on?'

I pull the T-shirt over my head. It fits, but it pinches a bit across my chest.

'There, that's so much better than all those tracksuits. Put your new shoes on.'

When Dad comes back, she presents me to him. 'Well? What d'you think?'

He gives me a strange look. I can tell he thinks I look crap but he's just being too polite to say. 'Like a princess,' he says, dropping a kiss on the top of my head as he pushes past us to go to the garage.

We're head to head on *Colin McRae Rally.*

'Why aren't you coming with us?' I ask.

He winces and takes the corner too sharply, spinning out into pine trees. I'm miles ahead of him now.

'I gave her a choice, Carmen,' he says.

I cross the finish line and win the game.

'Don't worry,' he says, switching off the machine without bothering to finish his lap. 'I expect she'll come to her senses soon.'

Last day of term is own-clothes day. Mum makes me wear my new outfit.

'You need to break it in,' she says. Then she looks at my feet and sighs. 'Look at the state of your toenails. I'll go and get my gloves.' She makes me sit on the bed while she cuts my toenails and files them. 'Darling, you know people say that you should never judge a book by its cover, but people do, they *do*. If you look like you care about yourself, then the world will care about you.' She puts spongy dividers between my toes, which make my feet feel funny. 'This colour will go really nicely, pearly pink, look.' She passes me the bottle. 'You do it.'

I have a very unsteady grip. My hands feel big and clumsy pinching the delicate brush, and besides it's hard to bend in half over my stomach. I wipe a stripe of polish on my new flares before I even get to my toenail. I manage my right foot, apart from my little toe, which I figure I can hide under the strap of the sandals, but by the time I've finished with my left foot the polish has started to congeal in blobby lumps.

Mum is narked when she comes back. 'Come on, hurry up.' I stand up in my shoes. She sighs. 'Don't pull the top down, you'll stretch it. Hold your stomach in. Wear your denim jacket over. That's better.'

'You copying me?' Janice asks. She's smoking a fag, hanging off Karl's arm. She's got the same top on as me. I pull the denim jacket close across my chest.

'No,' I say.

''S all right, only joking.'

We're supposed to be at end-of-year assembly. The first years have been practising a half-hour summer Micro Panto with the drama teacher all week.

'Micro pants, more like,' Janice says, giggling. 'We're going into town? You coming?'

Karl pulls his head back and looks at me like I'm a long way off. I know that he doesn't really want me hanging around.

'Go on then.'

I follow them out of the school gates as they walk in front of me hand in hand. When we walk past the alleyway that shortcuts behind the houses to the park, I duck down it. I bet they don't notice for ages I'm gone.

I sit on the swings until the dark clouds that have been gathering since first thing begin to drop down into the valley in a soggy veil of drizzle. It's supposed to be the start of summer, but it's colder than spring.

# 3

I know there's something wrong the minute I turn into the drive. Dad's car is parked with the boot right up to the side door. We're not supposed to be going until Dad gets back from America. The boot's flipped up and there are lots of boxes stowed, Mum's diet books and all her best suitcases.

She comes out of the house with another box in her arms.

'All right there, sweetheart.'

'What's going on?'

'We're going to Birmingham. You haven't forgotten already?'

She's too bright, too breezy. She's lying to me.

'I thought we were going next week.'

'No time like the present, Carmen. Seize the day,' she says. 'You only ever get one shot in this life.'

'But you've packed all your diet books.'

She dumps the box and looks at me, biting her lip. She tells me that we're not really going on holiday after all. We're going to live in Birmingham for a bit, just the two of us. For good.

She knocks on the door. 'Carmen! Come on, Carmen, sweetheart. Open up.'

'I want to stay *here*.' I can't believe she's really doing this. I thought she'd change her mind. She can't go now, not while Dad's away. If I can get her to wait till he gets back, she might change her mind.

'Carmen, I'm your mother. I'm not leaving you in an empty house all week.'

'Yes you can!' I say. 'I'll be fine. I'll wait for Dad. I'll explain, I'll tell him you've gone.' She hasn't packed half my stuff. My tracksuits, my best pair of trainers, all my posters.

She's smiling now, I know, even though I can't see her. 'You can talk to him when he gets back, OK?'

Not OK. None of this is OK. I know other people's parents split up, but they don't leave town. Rachel Veasy's mother moved her in with her new man six doors down the road from her old house.

'But *why* do we have to leave?'

'I'll tell you if you open the door.'

I sit down with my back against the door. It's all too fast.

'Why didn't you tell me before?'

'It just didn't seem *appropriate*. Besides, I wasn't sure myself until just now. I've just got to get out of here, Carmen. I've *got* to.' She taps on the door. 'We've got to go now. If we don't go now, I'll miss the moment. You'll understand when you're older, I promise you, you will.'

'But I want to stay here with Dad.'

'You can't stay here on your own.'

'Why not?'

'It's against the law. I'd get locked up.'

'So don't go then.'

'Carmen. Don't make this difficult.'

'But why can't you stay with Dad? Why? I don't want you to split up.'

She says she was going to tell me in the car. She's been offered the job in Birmingham. 'This is my chance, sweetheart, and your dad doesn't want me to take it. I know it's a big step, but it's exciting.' She's pleading with me now.

When I open the door she's rubbing her hands across her belly. She smiles at me, but there are tears glittering in the corners of her eyes. She grabs my hand. 'I know it's hard, sweetheart, I *know*, but you're just going to have to be a big girl.'

She hugs me, her arms hard and bony. 'It'll all be fine, you'll see. It's an adventure.'

*An adventure.* Adventures are supposed to be exciting. Like trekking in the Amazon, or crossing the desert, or climbing Everest. Birmingham's not an adventure, it's embarrassing.

She holds the steering wheel tight as we power round the bends on the road to the motorway. 'Don't look back,' she says. 'You'll turn to stone.'

She puts on the radio, it's Friday-night dance music, hyper, hyped-up beats. She turns it up and taps the steering wheel in time with the music, her wedding ring making a *click-click* against the plastic.

'Everything's changing, Carmen. We can't afford to stand still. *I* can't afford to stand still. I want a piece of the action. I'm not too old. I'm only thirty-five you know, that's not really very old at all.'

It seems ancient to me, but I don't say anything. The dark clouds that have been chasing us since Yorkshire finally block out the evening sun. It starts to rain and lorries throw up waves of spray as we pass them on the motorway.

'At least I got the car,' she says. 'At least I got the car.'

He'll go mad when he sees that it's gone. I squeeze my eyes together, really tight, and try to send a message to him. I want him to know that this wasn't my idea.

She starts going on about him and Moira. Repeating herself, on and on, like she can't stop. She says it's only fair that she should get something from Dad. That she can be a career woman too. The car is full of her voice, underlined by the droning of the engine.

'He doesn't think I can do it,' she says. 'He thinks I need him. I'll show him what I need.'

She turns to look at me, taking her eyes off the road.

All I can smell is the sickly leather off the seats, the whiff of exhaust fumes. 'I feel sick,' I say.

'For God's sake.' She pulls over sharply into the hard shoulder and leans across me to open my door. 'Do it outside, not in the car.' She pushes me, her hand against the small of my back. 'Go on. You shouldn't eat so much.'

Once I'm outside I don't feel sick any more. 'I'm all right now,' I say.

In the twilight the West Midlands twinkles like a fairground. The sky on the horizon is a murky pink and the air starts to smell of rubbish. The traffic gets heavier; more cars, headlights blinding us. We pass supermarkets, factories, warehouses, tower blocks. Everything is massive, much bigger than at home.

She says we're only going to stop with Nana and Grandad for a couple of days. 'I tell you, Carmen, a couple of days with those two is more than enough for anyone.'

31

As we get closer to Birmingham, the tower blocks close in around us. There are lights everywhere, tail lights, stop-go signs, street lights. It's like we're being pulled by a current, the car carried along by the momentum of the traffic towards the underpass.

I never imagined it would look like this. I thought it would be grey like an old photo, chimneys belching black smoke, sooty children playing in the dirt. Something in me fizzes.

'Look at it,' she says with a sigh. 'Whole world of opportunity.' She whoops and turns the radio up even louder. '*You gotta be yourself,*' she sings along with the music, '*and no one else.*'

Nana lives in Hall Green in the middle of a wide, winding street. Mum reverses into a space between a shiny red Toyota and a battered Nissan Sunny, hitting the kerb and swearing.

'Where do they live?' I ask, looking at the long, low bungalows that sit squatly on their patches of lawn.

'Over there,' Mum points across the road at a house half hidden by an unruly fern hedge. 'Behind all the greenery.' Long straggles protrude out into the road. 'It's your grandad,' she sighs. 'He's too bloody lazy to cut it.'

Nana's house has gold carpets and beige curtains. It smells funny, of damp or drains or old people, I don't know which. The kitchen is full of fake fruit: bananas, oranges, grapefruit, peaches, pears, plums. I can see the wind-up kiwi fruit I sent her for her birthday on top of the micro-wave. Even the fruit bowl with its sag of grapes is hard and shiny and made from moulded plastic.

Nana hugs me tight and holds me close, stroking my

hair. She smells of fags and cooking and cheap perfume. Her body is squashy as a cushion.

'You've grown so much.'

'She has,' Mum says. 'In the wrong direction.'

Nana has glasses with red frames that are too big for her face. They have the kind of lenses in that go darker in strong light. She's wearing a black cardigan that stretches over her bum. Around her waist is a bulge of fat that makes her look like she's wearing a rubber ring.

'Sit yourselves down. I've made tea.'

She gets a big tray of pizza out of the oven.

'It's only frozen, but they're quite nice these ones, got stuff in the crusts.'

'I'm on a diet,' my mother says, tapping open her cigarettes.

Nana frowns. 'You're not still going on about all that are you, Maria? Carmen, you'll have some tea, won't you?'

The light in the kitchen hurts my eyes. It's too bright, showing up all the veins under my skin. I have veins on my wrist that look like someone's drawn them with biro. If I touch them with my fingertips they make my toes feel funny.

'Where's Dad?' Mum asks.

'Where d'you think?' Nana cuts the pizza into uneven quarters. She puts a huge piece in front of Mum even though she acts as if it isn't there.

'You should be pleased he's not here, Maria. You don't want to hear the things he's been saying about you.'

'Shhh,' Mum says, nodding at me.

I smile at them and crunch into my pizza.

Nana makes me a bed in the lounge from the sofa

cushions because there's only one spare room and Mum's having that. Nana suggested we share the bed, but Mum turned up her nose.

'Just because I gave birth to her, doesn't mean I want to sleep next to her.'

The carpet smells funny and the cushions keep moving apart, making me slip down the gaps. When I fall asleep I dream of us in the car, driving on and on into the blackness, never stopping. Mum is talking to me but her voice has slowed down, distorted. She sounds like she's yawning, and when I turn to look at her she's got her mouth wide open. For a moment I think she's trying to swallow me.

I wake up suddenly, sitting upright, gasping for air. It's still dark and there are voices outside, a car engine turning over. Footsteps walk quickly then start running, a dog barks loudly next door. The air hums with noise, even now in the middle of the night. It's not like at home, where everything was so quiet; where if I listened too long to the silence I could convince myself that I was deaf.

# 4

The hedge is starting to block out the light. It's already grown halfway up the front windows.

'I tell him,' Nana says to Mum before he comes down for breakfast, 'but he won't do anything about it. It's depressing me.'

Nana has cooked a big breakfast of sausages, beans, bacon, eggs, and black pudding for Grandad. My mother makes a face when Nana puts a plate in front of her. Grandad coughs from behind his paper. He hasn't said a word to my mother yet.

'You all right then, Dad?' she says, sticking a menthol Superking between her lips.

Grandad looks at her over the top of yesterday's *Evening Mail*. 'Doing better than you, I expect. You left him for good?'

She bites her lip. 'Trial separation.'

Nana puts a plate of breakfast in front of me and snatches my mother's cigarette out of her mouth before she can light it. 'Not at breakfast, for God's sake, girl.'

Nana has given me a plateful of food: two sausages, two eggs, two bits of bacon and fried bread and beans. My mother raises her eyebrows at me and pushes her nose back so she looks like a pig.

'I'm going outside for a fag,' she says.

When she's gone the room is quiet except for the sounds of us eating: scraping forks across plates; Grandad grunting over his black pudding; Nana licking smears of ketchup from her lips. I look at my mother's food congealing on the plate.

'I knew it wouldn't last,' Grandad says putting his knife and fork down. 'That Brian's always fancied himself too much for my liking.'

'Ray, please, not in front of Carmen.'

They both look at me. I crunch on my last bit of fried bread, the meaty oil oozing out over my tongue. 'Can I have her breakfast?' I ask.

Mum has packed our old wicker picnic hamper with her food. A box of *Power Shakes*™, fat-free yogurts and spreads, rye crispbreads and bags of bran and apples that she boils up with sweeteners for breakfast. I watch her slicing an apple into thin slivers.

'You've got egg on your chin,' she says, wiping it off with a bit of kitchen roll.

'When can I see Dad?' I ask.

She narrows her eyes, puts a few heaped spoons of bran into her apples. 'You can ring him when he gets back.'

'You never told me you were *separating*,' I say, accusingly.

'I don't tell you everything.'

When he gets back I'll tell him I want to live with him. I don't want to stay here all my life. I want to hang out with Janice in the park, race Dad on *Wipeout*.

There are pictures of Mum all round Nana's house. Above the fire there's one of her wedding day. I'm in a little shiny dress with paper wings strapped to my back. I was meant to be a fairy but I've got my face scrunched up like I'm about to cry. My mother is beautiful: flowers coiled in her red hair, her dress a shimmery pea-green. Dad is in a morning suit, grinning and holding up a champagne glass.

'You know why he looks so bloody happy?' my mother says when she sees me looking at it. 'He was after my cousin Linda all through the reception. I should never have married him, Carmen.'

I stay in watching morning TV with Nana while Mum goes out to look at a flat. Nana watches lots of television. As soon as she gets up in the morning she puts it on. 'It's company,' she says.

We watch *Inch Loss Island* while we wait for *Trisha*. In this morning's episode Wendy, a contestant from Braintree, is crying because she misses her children. She's only lost a few pounds despite the fact that she's been on the island for a whole week and she's sticking rigidly to the programme's regime of nutritious, low-fat, calorie-counted meals.

The presenter's lipgloss shimmers as she tells how Wendy got fat when she was pregnant and how she's come to the island to get her figure back. 'It's probably water retention,' she advises. 'I expect the pounds will drop off next week.'

'Poor dab,' Nana says, cracking a Polo between her teeth. 'Nothing worse than a miserable fatso.'

Grandad comes in and stands in front of the telly. 'Pension day!' he says, flicking his book like it's raffle tickets. 'What you watching, bird?'

'Shhhh,' Nana's eyebrows furrow. Andrea from King's Lynn has lost nearly a whole stone.

'Women's telly.' Grandad tuts. 'See you later.'

'When the latch clicks Nana sighs. 'He lives down the pub these days,' she says, without taking her eyes off the screen. 'You don't want to get old you know bab, it isn't half boring.'

Next day Mum is really hyper. The flat she saw yesterday was in the wrong bit of town. 'Newtown, sweetheart, we don't want to live there, we'd get robbed every ten seconds and God knows what else.'

She's rung an old friend who's got a flat we might be able to stay in. She's put on lots of make-up and a tight dress to go and meet him. She looks like someone off the telly, her eyes sparkling, big gobs of gold jewellery on her ears. She hasn't done herself up like this for months, not even for work, and she looks strange, unreal, like it might all drop off her at any moment.

'It's all right,' she says, 'I'm going to rescue you from all this bloody food.' And she puts her arms wide to take in the whole of the house.

I look up from the TV and stare. All I can think is that she's wearing too much lipstick.

There's only racing and kids' programmes on. We watch *Sesame* Street for a bit, because Nana likes Big Bird. 'That's what I am now,' she says, 'a big bird.'

I must look really miserable because her face softens. 'Let's do something this afternoon. What d'you reckon? Fancy a trip uptown with your nan?'

We go on the bus, and it seems to take ages, bumping down the Stratford Road. Everything's a gaudy, grubby colour: curry houses, sari shops, butchers, grocers, video shops.

'They chop dogs up and put them in the food round here,' Nana says.

I look at a pasty carcass hanging in the window of a butcher's. 'Is that a dog?'

'Eugh, don't look.' Nana shudders. 'No, it's a goat. That's really disgusting, someone should complain.'

Further along the road, over the roundabout and down the last dip before town, the buildings get bigger, turn into ramshackle factories and warehouses. Car showrooms, tattoo parlours, a few dusty old pubs, Sparky's piano shop. In the sun the city looks steely: all glinting glass and pale concrete.

We go to the Bull Ring to look round the shops. Nana says they're going to pull it all down soon, build a more modern, posher shopping centre.

'It's a shame,' she says. 'It was beautiful when it was new.'

Everything is a quid, or two ninety-nine. She pulls me into Mark One.

'You want anything, bab? My treat.'

Untidy rails of clothes are laid out on the cracked lino. There is a kind of gallery with underwear and shoes and menswear, and below, down the thin, slippery steps a whole floor of ladies fashions. It smells of rubber and industrial glue and the assistants are hard and miserable in their red polyester overalls.

She pulls out a few things as we pass the rails. 'What about these?' She hands me a shiny blue dress and a black jumper made from the kind of cotton that bobbles when you wash it. I don't want to try on clothes; they'll only be too small or look crap.

'I'd rather have sweets,' I say.

Nana smiles at me. 'Orright, bab, let's go to the market first, eh? There's someone I'd like you to meet.'

To get to the Bull Ring markets we have to go down cranky old escalators. Beneath us is a huge underground hall, full of stalls with orange plastic signs announcing the stallholders' names in brown lettering. They sell everything: buttons, pet food, material, fresh fish, chickens, vegetables, books, T-shirts, leather jackets, eggs, shoes. The air smells strongly of fish and is filled with the noise of a constant hubbub of people shouting and talking. For a few seconds I am overwhelmed.

'Where are we going?' I ask, as Nana weaves her way in front of me through huddles of shoppers.

'To see Lisa. She's got a stall down here. You don't remember her, do you?'

'No.'

She looks at me and smiles. 'You were only a little scrap of a thing when you left.'

Right at the back, tucked away in one of the corners, next to a haberdashery stall and a fruit and veg stall, is a booth: The Nail File. The window is jewelled with little bottles. Hundreds of colours and textures. Pinks, lime greens, pine greens, purples of every shade, electric blues, glittery blues, silvers, golds, bronzes. There are more colours than I know names for.

The woman behind the counter is tall, and her hair is so black it has a blue sheen to it. Eyeliner sweeps under her eyes like Cleopatra's and her lipstick is a thick, shocking red.

'Hiya, Mum,' she says without looking up. 'Won't be a minute.'

She's painting something, concentrating really hard so the skin furrows between her eyebrows.

'You must be Carmen,' she tells me.

'How d'you know that?'

'I have amazing powers of perception. You ask your mum. I told her she'd come back here and now she has.'

'What are you doing?' I ask, too nosy to be shy.

'Ready-made extensions, then all I have to do is stick them on. There—' she says, showing me a tiny scrap of nail with a Caribbean sunset painted on it.

'It's gorgeous,' I say.

'D'you remember me?'

I shake my head. 'Sorry.'

'Don't be sorry. You were only a little babby when you left. Show us your hands.'

I look at Nana, but she's off chatting with the man on the haberdashery stall. *In Stitches* it says on the sign.

'You don't bite them, that's a good sign.' She picks up a file with a long, ivory handle. 'I'll do you a quick once over, then you can tell me about your mum. Is she all right? I heard she's been sick.'

Lisa files my nails with a deft, sawing movement. I don't know what to say. Her nails are a shiny red and hard like plastic. 'She's all right,' I say. 'She's got a new job.'

'You got a boyfriend then? I bet you've got loads, pretty thing like you.'

She's only being nice, I can tell, but I smile at her anyway. 'I'm into Madonna,' I offer.

'Are you now? Been around for a long while, her. You want a polish on that? I'll do you one for free. Pick a colour. Or you could have a transfer if you like, I've got some really pretty purple ones, look, with glitter in.' She

41

shows me some purple stars. 'They'd be good on a lilac background. What d'you reckon?'

'All right,' I say, not sure if I'm agreeing to something I'm not supposed to do.

She paints swiftly, accurately. Two strokes a nail. Then she sticks a purple star on each one and covers it with a quick brush of clear lacquer.

'Oooh, there's pretty,' Nana says. 'Proper little Spice Girl. We better go soon, let Lisa get on.'

'Hang on a minute, Mum, wait for them to dry.'

They talk about the Bull Ring, how it's a shame it's all coming down. But I'm not really listening; I'm admiring my nails. I wriggle them to make the glitter twinkle.

'Come back and visit, won't you?' Lisa says when we leave. 'Before they pull it all down? Tell your mum to come too.'

As we walk through the stalls to the escalators I hold my hands out in front of me; my fingers look magic, like wands with spells at the end of them.

Nana takes me to Druckers. On the ground floor, above the markets where there are no windows and no natural light. We sit at a table in the centre square, outside all the shops, next to a cluster of kiddie rides. There's a splat of melted ice cream on the window of the Postman Pat van.

She buys me a hot chocolate with a big blob of cream on top and a slab of fudge cake. She gets a pot of tea for herself and a chunk of apple strudel.

'I bought some for later,' she says, holding up a white box. 'Your mother's looking rather peaky, bit of sugar'll do her good.'

The cake is gorgeous, all gooey and chocolatey. To save my nails I have to hold the fork between my finger and thumb which makes it really difficult to eat.

Nana tuts when she looks at me. 'You've got it all over your face, love,' she says, spitting on a napkin and scrubbing my face with it.

I look at her lips, her lipstick is running into the lines round her mouth, her cheeks are sagging into pouches that hang off her jaw. Her hair is like a cloud; a puff of wispy grey hair stuck solid with hairspray. Mum says that Nana was a stunner when she was younger.

'Nana?'

'Yes, child?'

'You got any photos of before, when you were younger?'

'What you want to see them for? I don't like to look at them now,' she sighs. 'Once you lose your looks everything goes to the dogs.'

But she gets them out when we get back. Big, plastic-coated family albums with 'Treasured Memories' in gold on the cover. There are lots of my mother when she was a kid. Yellowy snapshots of her toddling on the beach, Nana in flowery dresses, her hair piled on top of her head in a beehive.

'That was in Great Yarmouth,' she says, pointing to a photo of herself in a blue satin minidress. 'I loved that holiday. Went out dancing every night. I made that dress an' all. Used to sew all my own clothes.' She runs her hands across the bulge of her belly.

Next to it there's a photo of Grandad leaning on a motorbike, fag in his hand, his hair flicked into a quiff like Elvis.

'Handsome once, wasn't he?'

Later there are photos of Nana and Grandad outside the house – 'That's what it looked like when we bought it, before he grew that bloody forest out there,' – and of my mother at fourteen in a pair of flares, hands on her hips, sticking her tongue out at the camera. 'Had some flesh on her then,' Nana says. 'Before all this dieting nonsense. Accused *me* of trying to make her fat, she did. Lisa blames herself but it weren't her fault. It was your mother. She never knew when to stop.'

She tells me that when they were girls, when my mum wasn't much older than me, they both went on a diet. That Lisa gave it up after a few months. 'She's like me, she likes her sweets too much. But your mum, she just got thinner and thinner. We didn't know what to do. It was driving us all mad. She got it into her head that she was fat—' she shakes her head '—she was thin as a stick. She's been funny about it ever since.' She turns the page of the book. 'Look at her there.'

It's a blurry snapshot that doesn't really look like Mum. She's holding a baby – me, I suppose – and bending backwards under the weight. She's so thin that there hardly seems to be any *body* there at all, just bones and clothes.

Nana puts her hand on my head, strokes my hair. 'Mind you don't listen to any of her nonsense, Carmen. I won't have you turning out like that.'

'I won't,' I say, looking at Mum. It makes me feel sick to see her like that.

At the back of the last book there is a little square photo, like the kind you get in photo-booths. The girl in the picture has spiky blue hair, eyeliner, black lipstick and a safety pin in her ear. Her expression makes her look like she's growling.

'Who's that?'

Nana looks over my shoulder and sighs. 'That,' she says, 'was our Lisa when she was seventeen.'

# 5

Mum doesn't like my nails. 'Too showy,' she says when she sees them. 'That was always her problem.'

Nana has unboxed the Druckers cakes and put them on a plate in front of us. I make a great dent in the soft wedge of sponge with my fork. Cream oozes out at the sides like shaving foam.

'We can't eat this,' Mum hisses at me. She unfolds a napkin. 'I'll wrap it up for later.'

I stop the fork halfway to my mouth, loaded with the rich, sticky, chocolate cake. Mum wrinkles her nose like it's something disgusting. Nana is coming back up the corridor. I put the fork down and scrape the rest of the cake reluctantly into the napkin. I've only had two mouthfuls.

'Give,' Mum says, snatching the parcel from me and stuffing it in her handbag.

'Finished already?' Nana sits down next to me. 'You want more?'

'Enough,' Mum says. 'We've been getting fat staying with you.' She prods her own arm with her finger. 'See? Fat.'

'That's skin, Maria.'

Mum pulls another cigarette from her packet.

'Carmen,' she says, looking straight at me. 'Go and get your things, there's a good girl.'

When I get back downstairs they are arguing.

'I don't know why you still won't see her. After all this time. Your own flesh and blood.'

'She was the one who stopped talking to *me*. I don't know what you were thinking of, taking Carmen down there, anyway. I don't want her getting ideas.'

Nana unfolds one of the napkins. It's a fancy one with *Vienna Patisserie* written in curly script. She puts it on the table, starts flattening the creases with the side of her hand.

'And you think that leaving Brian is a good idea, do you?'

The car is outside, half on the pavement like she parked it in a hurry.

'Honestly, that woman,' Mum says as she slides into the driving seat. Checking her face in the mirror, she wipes a smudge of lipstick from her top lip. 'If she had her way, we'd all be like elephants.'

I look at her and try to imagine what she was like before she had me. Her hair is long now, and wispy, usually pinned or tied up at the back. She dyes it a reddish-brown that says 'glossy radiance' on the bottle. She is smaller than the podgy girl in the photos.

'Mum,' I ask, 'what were you like when you lived here?'

She turns away from the mirror to look at me. 'A mess,' she says. 'And things were very different then. Weren't the opportunities that there are now. I never wanted to end up with what they've got.' She stabs her finger at the hedge. 'I mean, bless her, I know she's my mother but she's never had ambition. She'd be happy to see me get fat and work in Boots.'

'Wouldn't you be happy to see me work in Boots?'

'No, I wouldn't.' She turns the key in the ignition. 'You're lucky you are,' she says. 'Whole world of opportunity out there for your generation. You've got to grab it before you get old, before it's too late.'

Mum has found us a flat on the eighteenth floor of a tower block on the edge of the city centre. Sublet from someone called Billy; Mum tells me he's an old friend.

'You always know who your real friends are in a crisis,' she says.

'I didn't know there was a crisis.' I say, looking at the tower of flats that stretches up above us.

'Don't you get smart with me, madam.'

'There's broken windows,' I say, pointing to some windows higher up that are boarded over.

'They're doing them up, Carmen. This is prime property nowadays. Anyway, it's only temporary. Till I find somewhere we can buy. It'll be fun, like camping. What d'you reckon?'

'Suppose,' I say.

'You could sound a bit more enthusiastic.'

The lift is panelled with sheets of bubbled metal that bulge like the eyes of a fly. 'God, I look a *mess*,' Mum says, peering at her distorted reflection. The light is dingy and the floor is spotted with blots of chewing gum. I wrinkle my nose; it smells of pee.

'Cost a fortune, these flats,' she says, as we get out on floor eighteen. 'With all the redevelopment. They're going to do them up, Billy says, turn them into penthouses.' As if that explains everything.

We're number 128. With a metal door and a lock that you have to turn four times to open. The cream paint is chipped and the flap of the letter box is missing so you can see a square of pink carpet through the gap.

'Oooh, look at that view,' she says, as I follow her into the living room.

I have to hold my breath because the height makes me dizzy. The city spreads out underneath us, so far below that it looks like a toy town. The floor feels unsteady under my feet.

'I don't like it.'

'What d'you mean you don't like it? How can you not like it? Look at the view. You can see twenty miles from here. You'll get used to it.' She puts her hands on the glass, presses herself against it. 'This is where I should have been all along, Carmen. It's why I got depressed. I need to live, to be in the thick of it all.' She purses her lips and does a sort of slinky dance. 'I never wanted to settle down and have ki—' she stops herself, bites her lip. 'Never mind.'

I pretend not to notice.

Birmingham goes on for miles and miles. All the land up to the horizon is filled with buildings and roads. I don't want to stand too close to the window. I'm scared I might fall off.

'Look,' she says, pointing. 'Over there, that's where the Power House used to be. We used to go there on nights out. Billy's band did a gig there once. But that was about as far as it went.' She laughs. 'Birmingham wasn't very sophisticated in those days. Not like now. You know things have changed so much in the last ten years, it's amazing.'

The flat has two bedrooms with windows that face out on to the city, a lounge with a small kitchen and a bathroom. There's a balcony, the door leading out of Mum's bedroom. It's windy, the air howling round us, like it wants to pick us up and throw us off, send us flying out into space. Mum puts her arms out.

'Oooh, isn't it bracing?'

I stand with my back to the wall, edging out, inch by inch, as if I'm on a small ledge, not a balcony. The noise of the wind and the traffic is deafening.

'It's all right, sweetheart, you won't fall off. Look.' She pushes against the balcony, lifting herself up off her feet.

'*Mum!*' My heart sinks to my stomach. 'I don't like it.'

The wind blows her hair across her face, into her mouth. '*I don't like it.* Afraid I'd jump off, were you? Bless.' She gives me a pitying look.

There's hardly any furniture, only one bed, and a mattress on the floor in what Mum says is my room. No TV, no phone, and only a small, uncomfortable futon sofa. There are thick, pink, nylon curtains to match the carpet. Mum makes a face at them. 'We'll have to do something about those.'

I help her get our stuff out of the car. It takes ages to get everything up in the lifts. 'We won't be here for ever,' she says. 'It's just a stop gap, a stepping stone.'

She unpacks all her cleaning things from one of the boxes.

'Billy's not very houseproud. I can cope with scruffy if I have to, but I can't deal with unhygienic.' She gives me some bedding. 'Here, go and do your bed.'

She plugs the stereo in, tunes the radio to Choice FM. I can hear her from my bedroom, doing karaoke in the kitchen, trying to sing all the high notes with Mariah Carey and Whitney Houston.

There isn't a wardrobe or anything, so I can't really unpack. I arrange my trainers in a row against the wall. I didn't even bring any posters to put on the walls.

'You know what's so great about having our own place is that there isn't any *food*,' she says, using a Brillo pad to scrub the grill pan. She looks up at me, wipes hair out of her eyes with her wrist. 'Makes everything so much *easier*.'

Later she makes tea from her hamper. Weight Watchers beans on toast for me. Fat-free yogurt with four table-spoons of bran for her. We sit on the futon, side by side. She eats her yogurt slowly with a teaspoon, putting the spoon in her mouth again and again, sucking the yogurt off with her lips a layer at a time. She's only on her third teaspoon by the time I've finished my beans.

'Here,' she says, handing me the pot, still nearly full, to throw away. 'I'm not hungry.'

Out come her catalogues and magazines. Her new job starts in a week and she says she needs to familiarize herself with their range. She spreads them on the carpet in front of her and kneels down in front of them, making notes. The clothes are cheaper than Mrs Walton's but still quite expensive. All their winter coats are over a hundred pounds. The classy end of the high street, Mum says, the kind of place that sells suits for work and dresses for cocktail parties.

'You know, *Linda* looked fantastic in a Galliano version of that frock in Milan.' She points to one of the dresses in the catalogue. 'She's pregnant, you know, and she still

51

looks amazing. Mrs Walton's met her at the shows once. Said she was every bit as beautiful as her photographs.' She pauses. 'Bitch.'

She goes quiet and I ignore her, flicking through her magazines instead, looking at all the clothes, the make-up, the silky faces and shiny skin.

'We'll be like sisters, you and me,' Mum says, smiling. 'City slickers.' The radio has started playing trance music, all strings and chorus; she turns it up and lights another menthol Superking.

Even with the curtains shut my room isn't properly dark. I put my head underneath them and hold on tight to the window ledge. The clouds are pink with the reflection of the city lights. I hold my nails up and watch the stars sparkle against the window, wriggling them until they look like part of the sky.

I lie down again but I can't sleep. There's too much noise. I can pick out individual sounds, brakes squealing, cars revving, people shouting, the wind gusting, every now and then air whistling through the cracks in the walls. I'm just drifting off when a loud buzzing noise starts, and doesn't stop; though sometimes it seems to move further away. I get up and look out the window. It's a helicopter. I can feel my heart start to beat faster. There must be something bad happening.

I knock on her door. '*Mum*? What's going on?'

She doesn't answer, so I open the door; she's asleep, a mask over her eyes. Her sleeping pills are on the side by the clock radio. The buzzing outside seem to be getting louder and louder. I shake her.

'Mu-*um, Mum.*'

She stirs. 'Ngh, what is it?' she says, her voice thick with sleep.

'Outside, there's a helicopter.'

She lifts her eye mask up and blinks at me. 'Police, darling, don't worry about it, now . . .' She settles herself back on the bed and seems to fall asleep again.

'But Mu-*um*.' I pinch her arm but she doesn't flinch.

The noise has gone further away but I can hear it coming back. It seems to be circling. I go back to my room and look out of the window, wrapping myself in the curtain. I can see it in the distance, swarming like a fat black insect, breaking up the darkness with its searchlight.

# 6

In the morning she laughs at me for being frightened of the helicopters. 'Scaredeycat,' she says. 'You'll have to toughen up a bit. Get *streetwise*.'

She sits me down on the futon, gently pressing my shoulders with her fingers, whispering now. 'You know, I realized something a long time ago. If you feel anything, anything at all, for whatever reason, even the smallest little twinge, and you think, oh no, I'm going to start crying, or I'm going to go and eat something I shouldn't, squeeze your stomach muscles together really tight, or bite your lip, or dig your fingernails into your palms. Control it. Don't let anyone see that you're upset. That way you'll always win. *Always*.'

When I look up, her expression is invincible.

She gives me some hydro-repair anti-ageing cream to rub under my eyes, so they won't look red and swollen. While she brushes my hair she tells me about Billy. She says she wants me nice because he hasn't seen me since I was in a pram.

'Don't want him thinking I haven't been looking after you,' she says.

I've chipped my nails. One of the stickers has come off, leaving a star-shaped hole in the polish. I pick at it while

I wait for Mum to finish her make-up. My skin is tired and prickly. We haven't even had breakfast yet.

'Don't talk to me now, I'm concentrating.'

We're stalled at a junction. Cars sound their horns, buses squeal as they brake behind us. Mum is going hot and red, turning the key in the ignition again and again. 'I told Brian it needed a service.'

When we're moving again, zipping towards Five Ways, she asks me how much I think the car is worth.

I shrug. I don't really know how much cars cost. Loads, I expect. She tells me that it's worth thirty thousand new. Second-hand it ought to fetch ten, twelve. 'Keep us going for a month or two.'

'I thought we were only borrowing it.'

'He can always buy another one,' she says, running a red light. 'It's only what I'm owed.'

We turn a corner off the main road, down a narrow side street. At the end is a wooden-clad pub that stands on the brow of the hill looking down over a big, leafy park. There's bunting tied from the roof to the telegraph poles and a big red and gold banner above the door that says:
*Steers. All U Can Eat. £10.*

Chalkboards propped up by the door announce the attractions: BIG SCREEN SPORTS. FRIDAYS KARAOKE.

We park the car in the Staff Only space. 'Well, here we are,' she says, yanking the handbrake.

Bolts slide across the door. He's wearing leather trousers, cowboy boots and a dirty white shirt with a crumpled leather waistcoat. His spiky black hair flops over his eyes and he rubs a fat hand over his gut. The air around him stinks of chips and cigarettes.

'Orright, Maria, thought you were the cleaner.'

'Hello, Billy,' Mum says, sounding a bit put out. 'What's this then? Your *Boon* look, is it?'

'Ha ha.' He hugs her clumsily, grabbing her arm to keep his balance.

'Mind the jacket, it's Versace,' she says, wiping her sleeve as if she's dusting him off. 'This is Carmen.'

He bends down to look at me. His skin is pale and freckled; I'm sure he has eyeliner round his eyes. I get a waft of stale breath. 'You're a beauty, aren't you?' His voice is really raspy, like he's got a throat full of sandpaper. He pulls a strange expression. 'Just like your mum.'

Mum touches his arm. 'Don't be a tease.'

'Come in, come in.' He stands back from the door.

Inside is a huge, square barn of a room. Everything is made of logs. There are logs for chairs, logs for tables, even the walls are made of logs sawn in half and nailed to the bricks. There are pictures of lakes and mountains and pine forests on the walls, and a servery built to look like an outdoor barbecue, together with flame-effect lighting that flickers over the bark of the fake-log fire.

'I tell you, Maria, best thing I ever did getting into this game. Everyone round here's pissed off with curry.'

'It's certainly a surprise, Billy.'

'Entrepreneurial, Maria, that's what I am now. Entrepreneurial.'

We follow him across the restaurant to the bar. The tables are covered with scrunched napkins, plates, bottles, ashtrays, glasses, baskets of cold chips, even, on one, party hats and streamers.

'Scuse the mess,' Billy says, side-stepping a chicken wing.

Stools covered in cowskin material stand haphazardly around the bar. There's a stuffed buffalo head behind the bar, glass eyes glistening. Billy sees me looking and pats it on the nose.

'Fancy a drink? Pernod and black, like old times?' He pushes a glass against the optics. 'I used to go to school with your mother, Carmen,' he says. 'Didn't she tell you?'

'Don't start, Billy,' Mum says.

We sit at the only clean table in the place. Still set with knives and forks and napkins. It's a big, round table made from a sawn piece of trunk. Sap has risen through the varnish, making sticky bobbles on the surface. Billy comes over with a bottle of Coke and two Pernods. He downs his in one, making a face after he's swallowed it.

'Agh,' he says, shaking his head. 'That's better. You been to see Lisa yet?'

Mum shakes her head. 'One step at a time, Billy. Besides, she knows where to find me.'

'I have,' I say, holding up my nails.

'Oooh, there's pretty.' He cocks his head to one side, his black hair flopping over his eyes and looks at Mum. 'Why didn't you stay in touch?' He reaches a fat hand across the table but Mum pulls hers away, puts them in her lap.

She shrugs and looks at me. 'Things changed,' she says.

Billy takes a cigarette out of her packet. 'Haven't lost all yer bad habits though.'

The doorbell rings; this time it is the cleaners. Three women in blue overalls come in. They go out the back, start clanking around, getting Hoovers out of the cupboards, shaking out plastic sacks.

I look at Billy as he walks back to the table. He swaggers a bit in his boots, though his trousers are too tight for him. He looks like he could be famous. I don't know anyone at home who looks like him. I am amazed that Mum knows him at all. He looks like the kind of man she would sneer at on the street. He keeps giving me funny looks, when he thinks I'm not looking – perv.

'What about the car then?' Mum says. 'Can you shift it for me?'

Billy lights his fag. 'I can give you five thousand for it, Maria. Cash,' he says, his voice full of smoke.

'Oh, c'mon, Billy, it's worth loads more.'

'Not without papers it's not. Take it or leave it.'

Mum looks at me out of the corner of her eye, and takes a sip on her Pernod.

'All right then,' she says.

When we leave, Billy gives her an envelope full of twenty-pound notes. She stuffs it in her handbag.

'I've taken your first two months' rent out of that. Don't tell me I don't know how to look after you, Maria.' He winks. 'I always knew you'd come back. Country life doesn't suit you, gel, this is where you belong. Come and have your tea later if you like. On the house.' He kisses her on the cheek, puckering his lips like a suction pad. The kiss leaves a wet trail on Mum's cheek, which glistens as she steps out into the sunlight.

'Wouldn't eat there if you paid me,' Mum says, turning up her nose as the door clunks shut behind us. She insists that we walk back into town. She says it's not far and that we need the exercise. It's miles. All down the main road, traffic screaming around us, Mum walks really fast, and I get out of breath trying to keep up with her.

We walk past houses and offices and restaurants and

off-licences and chip shops. Mum has her face set, her head down, her shoulders hunched. People step out of our way as we come towards them.

My sandals are rubbing my feet and by the time we get to Broad Street I have to stop.

'It hurts,' I say, looking at the trickle of blood on my heel.

Mum sighs. 'Well I haven't got any plasters. Here, try a bit of tissue.' She folds up a square of bog roll and pushes it under the strap.

It works for a bit but then it falls off again and we have to go into Boots for plasters.

Bending down in the shop to stick the plaster on, she mutters at me, 'If you weren't so heavy, Carmen, you wouldn't put so much pressure on your feet.'

In town we buy a toaster and a kettle and some curtains and a couple of table lamps. Mum says she doesn't want to go mad, but it seems like we buy something in every shop. At the cash desk, Mum gets her wad of money out and peels off notes like she's in a gangster film or something. On the way to Marks and Spencer we pass her new workplace. A narrow little shop with a tall front window. There's summer wear in the window. Strappy tops, shorts, mini skirts, wrap-around frocks that look like sarongs, string handbags, sandals.

She makes me wait outside while she goes in. I can see her at the back of the shop, shaking hands with one of the sales assistants. When she comes out she's beaming. 'Good to get your feet under the table as soon as you can in this line of work.'

We go to the Pavilions and spend ages in The Pier choosing candlesticks, tea towels, a novelty toast rack.

59

We're standing outside McDonald's, Mum trying to decide whether we should go to Rackhams to look at their steamers. 'It's so much healthier than boiling, and you know it was the one thing I forgot to pack.'

'Mum, I'm *starving.*' I wasn't going to say anything, but it's nearly three and there's still no sign of her stopping for food. 'Can I have a Big Mac?'

She shrugs. 'If you want to behave like a pig.' She stares at me.

'I want a Big Mac,' I say again, staring back. She gives me a fiver.

'I'll meet you back here in ten minutes.' Her mouth twists shut, making her look mean. 'Miss Piggy.'

# 7

There's a battered looking Ford Fiesta parked at the bottom of the tower on the double yellow lines, big patches of rust up the back, a dented side panel. As we pass it, the horn goes. Someone puts their head out of the window.

'Maria! Carmen!'

It's Dad.

He gets out of the car. His clothes are creased, he's got his tie knotted halfway down his chest, his hair's ruffled. He looks like he hasn't shaved for a few days. Mum just stops when she sees him, hides her shopping bags behind her legs.

'Brian,' she says, her voice all tight and funny. 'Who told you I was here?'

'I want the car, Maria.'

'Too late, I sold it. And I've spent the money. Looks like you got yourself a new one, anyway.' She nods at the car and smirks.

Dad says he's worried about her, that he wants her to come back.

'Should have thought about that before.' Mum holds out her hands to him. They're trembling. 'Look!' she says. 'Look! It's you that's done this to me, Brian. You. It may have escaped your notice but I actually *had* a life before I met you.'

Dad looks at me. 'Wasn't me that wanted it to be like this.'

Mum gives me her handbag. 'Go let yourself in, sweetheart.'

He never raises his voice, even though he has plenty of reasons to shout. It's Mum who does all the screaming. I can hear her calling him names as I get into the lift. Dad's voice is low and sad and tired, like he knows it's not worth arguing.

When I get into the flat I go out on the balcony, biting my lip to stop myself feeling scared. I peek over quickly, in case the concrete gives way. I can't see them, though the car's still there, a big rust patch on the roof.

She comes out on to the balcony, stalks up and down, her heels clack-clacking on the concrete.

'He wants a word with you,' she says, puffing out her cheeks, her hands on her hips.

We sit in the car listening to the radio, Dad chain-smoking cigarettes. I don't know what to say to him.

'Bought *Grand Turismo* the other day,' he says, eventually.

'Turbo or normal?' I ask.

'Didn't know there was a difference.'

I roll my eyes. 'Like, Dad, it's been in all the magazines. The turbo version is *loads* better.'

'Uh, I guess I wasn't concentrating when I bought it,' he says. Then he clears his throat and asks me if Mum's looking after herself.

'Is she eating?'

'Stupid question,' I say. 'Next.'

He tells me that he knows it's all a bit of a mess. 'But it's not your fault, you know that, love. No one's cross with you.'

'Can I come back with you?' I say. 'I hate it here.'

He says he understands it's difficult but that I have to be grown up about things. 'Your place is with your mother. Someone's got to look after her.'

'Don't you like me any more?' I ask. Tears prick behind my eyes. A little sob escapes that I try to stifle with a cough. I dig my fingernails into my hands.

'Oh, of *course* I do. It's just complicated. You'll understand when you're older. Everything will be all right, you'll see.' He gives me his card with his mobile number on it, tells me to call him any time. 'Any time.' Then he takes out a wad of notes. 'Here, take this. Spend it on something nice. Get yourself a new pair of trainers.'

'Mum won't let me wear them,' I say, miserably.

'New trousers or something. I don't know. Keep it secret, then you can spend it on what you like. You're turning into a pretty girl now; you'll be making friends here soon enough. Everything will be OK, you'll see.'

'Don't say that!' I say to him. 'You don't know fuck all.'

'Carmen!' He looks at me, shocked. 'Don't swear at me, please.'

I get out of the car. 'I can do what the fuck I like. You're not my dad.'

I look at him, expecting him to be cross, but his eyes are soft, watery. He looks like he's trying not to cry.

'You're becoming just like your mother,' he says.

'And you can have your poxy money back.' I throw the notes at the car, the wind catches them, sending them skitting across the pavement into the gutter.

63

As I open the door to the flats I hear an engine turning over, then finally pulling away. When I look behind me there's an empty space where the car used to be as if he's just vaporized. Upstairs, Mum's door is shut and when I knock there's a muffled 'go away'. I lie on my bed and try so hard not to cry that my face feels hot and itchy.

The noise of the intercom buzzing makes my heart jump nearly out of my chest. For one moment my heart leaps. I think it might be Dad, changed his mind, come back to get me.

'Lerrus in, love.' It's Billy's gravelly voice.

When he appears at the door he looks better than he did this morning, cleaned, shaved, though he's still wearing leathers and cowboy boots. He's carrying a portable TV.

'Just thought I'd drop by, see how you were settling in. Brought you a telly. Found it in Izzy's round the corner, only cost a tenner. Works OK and everything.'

He bustles past me into the lounge. 'Where's your mother then?' he asks.

'Sleeping,' I say.

He puts the telly on the floor in the lounge and starts to tune it in.

'You can get one, two, three and four, but not five,' he says. 'Telly's too crap for that. I said to your mum, mind, if she wants to get Digital I can sort that out for her on the cheap. More channels 'an that, it's better, isn't it?'

He chatters at me like this for quite a bit while he fiddles with the switches and bangs the side to get the picture to hold. I stand over him and watch.

'There you go,' he says, 'no remote control though.

You'll have to get up to change channels.' He looks up at me from the floor.

'Thanks,' I say, hoping that he won't notice that my face is blotchy.

Billy smiles at me. 'No problem, kiddo. I'll just go and look in on your mum.'

He goes into her room without knocking. I can hear his trying-to-be-quiet voice rasping over the sound of the telly. When he comes out he shuts the door really gently and tiptoes back into the lounge.

'Your mum's a bit poorly,' he says, as if I didn't know that already. 'What d'you reckon to coming over the restaurant for a bit? I said to her I'd feed you.' He smiles at me awkwardly, showing his stained teeth. 'Won't bite you. Promise.'

I shrug. 'Whatever,' I say.

As we walk down the road to his silver BMW, Billy spies something in the gutter. 'Finders keepers,' he says, holding up a twenty-pound note. 'Some joker will be sorry to lose that.' He folds it up and slips it in his pocket.

His mobile phone goes, playing the tune to *The Great Escape*.

'Orright? Lisa! You orright? Yeah . . . Nah, I've got Carmen with me. Yeah . . . Yeah . . . Yeah . . . yeahyeah orright orright, I know I know. See ya later.' He flips it shut. 'Great things. mobile phones. D'ya want one? I can get you one cheap.'

'No thank you,' I say, primly. 'Mum says they give you cancer.' I think of the picture that she showed me in a magazine once, a girl with a cancer around her ear big as a cabbage.

'Do everything your mum says, do you?'

He smirks and ruffles my hair. I wonder what Dad would say if he saw Billy. He might let me go home with him then.

We drive around for ages. Billy's got a few errands to run. He parks up outside a big warehouse. 'I won't be a sec,' he says, grabbing a scruffy Adidas bag off the back seat.

I sit in the dark, trying not to get scared. The road is empty apart from a few cars and the occasional bus that comes chugging up the long hill out of town. In the glove compartment I find lighters, a few tapes, a mobile-phone charger. I rummage for sweets but there's only scrunched-up Burger King wrappers and ticket stubs from the football.

He taps on the window, making me jump. 'Having a good nosy? You're just like your mother.'

Quickly, I push the flap of the compartment shut.

'Sorry,' I mumble. But he laughs.

I try not to look at him as he gets in the car. He sits down with a sigh, his breath dark with cigarettes. I pull my denim jacket across my chest, wriggle my toes in my sandals so the blisters don't show. He could be taking me *anywhere*.

The room looks like it hasn't been cleaned in months. There's things everywhere: records, CDs, videos, cigarette packets, ashtrays, empty cans of Coke and Tennents Extra, vodka bottles. The carpet's covered in shreds of tobacco and ripped Rizla packets.

He's ordered takeaway pizzas and burgers and chips from Zaff's using his mobile. He said he couldn't be arsed to drive back to the restaurant. 'Same old shit wherever you buy it.' His flat is just out of town in a place I've not been before, Balsall Heath. It's a whole upstairs of an old Victorian house.

I sit on the edge of the sofa with the plate on my knees.

'What 'm ah thinking? I'll get you a knife and fork.'

He pulls the coffee table towards us, wiping the mess on to the floor. 'Sorry 'bout the mess, we had a bit of a sesh last night. Bit different to what you're used to this, isn't it? What was your house like before?'

Clean, I think, looking at the carpet. 'Nice,' I say to him.

'What? Not any more than that? Just nice?'

I look away from him and dig into my plate, starting with the burgers which are cold by now. 'Thank you for the food,' I say.

''S all right. Your mother's a good friend of mine.'

He eats really quickly. Shovelling the food in, swallowing, before it's chewed properly. His mobile goes, he answers it, still chewing on a bit of pizza.

'Orright? Naaah, mate, sorry I'm a bit tied up right now . . .' He looks at his watch. 'Nother coupla hours? Yeah. No, not now, I've got someone here like.' He laughs, spitting crumbs on the carpet. 'No, not like that. Yeah, yeah, see ya later.' He puts the phone on the table and switches it off. 'Bastard things.'

A stereo takes up nearly the whole of one corner, a stack of black boxes with little lights and knobs. There are loads of speakers spread out around the room. Behind it a guitar and an amplifier.

'Used to be in a band when I knew your mother,' Billy informs me. He gets up. 'I'll show ya something now.' He flips through a pile of records. 'Here y'a,' he says, handing me a record.

*Distress* it says in metallic blue zig-zag writing over the top of a black-and-white photograph of a group of punks. I don't recognize him at first, he looks so young. Like someone I could go to school with.

'Is that you?' I ask, pointing to the boy in the middle, his hair cut in a short crop, a shirt and a skinny tie half undone round his neck.

'Handsome, wasn't I?'

On the back there's a collage of photos, badges, tickets, posters. One badge says SPEED FREAK, another EVERYBODY'S WEIRD.

'Those are the songs,' he says. 'Clever, isn't it? Lisa did it. There's your mum, look.' He points to a photo of two girls. 'And Lisa.' They're both done up all goth, lots of big hoops in their ears. 'Inseparable they were. Your mum thought the world of Lisa back then. Bet she never told you that.'

It gives me a funny feeling to look at it and I give the record back to him.

'We only ever did that record and a few gigs down the Barrel Organ, but we were good when we were around. Our drummer worked with UB40 after. I'd play it fer ya but my decks're cabbaged. Lisa and Mar— sorry, your mum, were our number-one fans.'

He presses a button on the remote control, reggae booms through the speakers. He nods his head to the lazy beat.

'C'mon finish up, you haven't eaten all yer tea.'

'I'm full,' I say, lying back on the sofa.

'You don't want any ice cream?'

I shake my head and squash my lips together. I look at my feet; they're dirty, black sooty streaks across my toes.

'You don't say much, do you?'

He gets up and tidies up a bit, shaking out a black bin bag and filling it with cans, bottles, the rest of my food. 'I tell ya, we throw away so much food in the restaurant. It's criminal. I need a dog I do.' He lights a fag, jigs about a bit to the music. 'When I was your age I was a skinny little runt. Footie. That was all I cared about. What you into then? Boy bands? Trainers? PlayStation? I dunno, what are kids into these days? I'm out of touch.'

I shrug. I wish he'd put the telly on and shut up. He rubs his stomach awkwardly. 'Well. Look. If you don't mind, I'm just going to get changed. Here, you watch the telly.'

I know that really he's gone to smoke some weed. I can smell it coming out of his room when I go to the toilet. In my old school the boys smoked it all the time, in lunch breaks down the bottom of the playing fields, rolled up in crappy little joints. When the police came round school to give us an anti-drugs talk, Jason Myers rolled a fake one and threw it at the policeman halfway through his speech. We all thought he would get into trouble but the policeman just picked it up and looked at it and said that no one was going to get very high if they rolled joints like they were Tampax wrappers.

When he comes back, his eyes are red and half-closed. He sinks into the sofa next to me. 'I tell ya,' he says. 'I'm saving up. I'm gonna get off out of here one of these days. Get a bar in Spain. Just imagine it, always sunshine, sea views, cheap beer, cheap fags. Not fair is it, work?'

Later, outside the doors of our block, he digs in the back pocket of his trousers.

'Here y'a,' he says, giving me the twenty-pound note

he found in the gutter. 'Buy yerself summat nice with that.'

When Mum answers the buzzer he touches me lightly on the shoulders. 'I won't come in, I've got things to do. See you soon, eh?' I watch him go back to his car, the street lights reflecting off his leather trousers as he walks.

'Didn't he want to come up for a drink?' Mum asks. She's up now, all the lights on. She's cleaning the kitchen, scrubbing the floor with Ajax. 'I wanted to tell him that he should have got someone in. This place is filthy.'

She wipes a wisp of hair from her eyes and stands up. I can tell that it makes her dizzy because she has to cling on to the units and her eyes roll back in her head. She takes a deep breath. 'I'm so glad we're here though. Aren't you? Things are really looking up for us now. Was Billy all right? Did you get on?'

I think about the picture of her and Lisa, the record and Billy's flat. It's like she's a different person all of a sudden and not my mother at all. ''S all right,' I say, shrugging.

She sighs. 'Sweetheart, sometimes I wonder if you've got any personality at all.'

# 8

The night before she's supposed to start work, she's up all night. Pacing the flat, writing letters, flipping through magazines. I fall asleep to the sound of her *Pete Tong Essential Mix* on repeat, the bass line thudding into the carpet.

She wakes me at six. I'm supposed to be spending the day with Nana and I'm going over on the bus on my own. Mum said she'd drive me but she hasn't got a new car sorted out yet.

'I'm so nervous,' she says. 'I can feel my heart going.' She puts her hand on her chest. 'Bird in a cage.'

She follows me round the flat while I get dressed, babbling on to me about how excited she is, about how she's going to make it work for her, about how this time next year she'll be a real success story. 'You better believe it, girlfriend,' she says in a silly voice.

'I believe you,' I say.

On the way to Nana's I get lost. I get off at the right bus stop but turn down the wrong street. All the roads look the same, miles of bungalows and low, squat semis with big puffballs of privet outside.

*Privet, Keep Out.* I put that on my door once when I was younger. Dad laughed at my spelling and said not to worry, that maybe I'd turn out to be good at maths or something.

I have to walk back the way I came and down another road until I can see the mess of greenery that now half hides Nana's house. The wispy fern tips are stretching up towards the roof.

Nana's persuaded Grandad to get Sky Digital. She's watching *Classic Coronation Street* on Granada Plus. 'It's the really good episodes with Pat Phoenix in,' she says, rushing back to the TV. She shows me the remote control, a keypad with tens of tiny buttons. 'You can send email with that,' she says. 'Your lifetime will be amazing you know, Carmen.'

She asks me how Mum's getting on. I tell her that I've met Billy.

'Have you now?' She raises her eyebrows. 'Your mother used to be really soft on him.'

'He's renting us the flat,' I tell her.

'Thought as much,' Nana mutters under her breath before changing the subject. 'There's scones on the side in the kitchen. Help yourself. I bought them for you.'

Nana's house is stuffy in the heat. Because of the bushes there's no breeze, and though it's cooler than outside it's humid and manky, and smells like gone-off milk.

I put the light on in the kitchen; it's like twilight otherwise. Bags of cakes are heaped up on the side: scones, slab cakes, bread puddings, jam tarts. I take a couple of scones and a piece of bread pudding into the lounge.

'Ooh, give us a bit of that,' Nana says, stretching across and digging her fingers into the moist, fruity mush and breaking off a chunk for herself. 'Mmm.' some of it falls on to her dress and she doesn't even notice.

I look at the mess on my plate and suddenly I don't feel very hungry. I eat it anyway because there's nothing else to do.

After we've worked our way through the cakes and a few more advert breaks, Nana starts talking about lunch. 'I think we should have chips for a special treat. What d'you think?'

I look at my nails; there's only one little fleck of purple left.

'Can I see Lisa?' I ask.

Nana sighs. 'If I were fitter, love, I'd take you into town like that –' she clicks her fingers '– but it's my knees, they're playing up today. The chip shop's about as far as it goes these days.'

Really, it's because Agatha Christie films are on the classic cinema channel all afternoon.

She sends me out to get chips. It's boiling out. A proper summer day. Last year me and Janice spent the whole holidays outside her house getting suntans, or down the park smoking fags while we rubbed in our sun cream. Mum told me off when she saw I'd burned my neck. 'Silly girl, you'll get skin cancer.'

At the chip shop I think, I could just get the bus uptown, go and see Lisa and then come back, I bet Nan would never notice. I grasp the fifty pences until they mark my hand. I daren't. I get double portions of chips and two pieces of cod and an extra battered sausage for Nan.

'Ugly family, aren't we?' Mum says. She's picked up one of Nan's photos and she's studying it closely. It's one with Nana and Grandad and Lisa and Mum outside the house in Stirchley where Mum grew up. Lisa is leaning sulkily against the wall, hiding under her fringe, and Mum is grinning, her front teeth missing. 'Look at my double chin,' she says and puts the photo back with a sneer.

'Come on then, madam.' She swings a new set of car keys round her finger. She's bought a second-hand VW Golf. 'I'll take you for a test drive.'

'You sure you won't stay for tea?' Nana comes out of the kitchen with a tray of tea and cakes.

'Mum, I told you, we don't have time. You'll be drinking that by yourself.' She bustles me out of the door but tells Nana that she'll have to look after me for the rest of the week. Nana thinks this is great.

'*Falcon Crest* day on Carlton tomorrow,' she shouts after me like it's something I'll be pleased to know.

Janice sends a letter on Friends Forever notepaper. Dad must have given her our address.

*Hiya Babe.* She's miserable, Karl's dumped her and taken his mobile back. *I miss you. Everything's boring here. What's the talent like in Birmingham????!!!! Can I come and visit? Are you going to school down there?*

She's left her number at the top of the letter, but when I give her a ring no one answers.

I start a letter back, drawing nail shapes round the top and filling them in with swirly designs. *Dear Janice, Birmingham's great*, I write.

I tell her to forget about Karl and come and visit. That we can go shopping and get our nails done. Then it all comes out in a rush of words, all about Mum and Dad: how I can't go back to Yorkshire, how Mum is being a cow, how I hate her, how I want to run away.

Reading it back, it sounds wrong. I Tippex over *great* and write *weird* instead.

I don't post it.

On the wall, behind her seat, along with all the sparkly packets of transfers and jewels, and gilt-edged Spanish fans and postcards of flamenco señoras and pictures of matadors, is a photo of a girl with purple hair and silver eyeshadow. She's holding her nails up to the camera, silver swirls over a purple colour the same as her hair.

'Who's that?' I ask.

'Debra,' Lisa says. 'Taught me everything I know. This was her stall before, but she went off to Jamaica on me.' She sucks her teeth. 'I'm saving up to go and visit.'

I'm not supposed to be here. Mum thinks I'm in the flat watching TV on my own. I'm sat up on the high stool, at the Nail File. Around us the market is closing up for the day. There's not many shoppers, and boards are being put up against the stalls and padlocked.

'When d'you start school?' Lisa asks.

'Next week.'

I bite my lip; I've been trying not to think about it.

She asks me which school I'm going to and when I tell her, she laughs. 'Broadhurst in Kings Heath, is that where she's sending you? She always wanted to go there when we were kids because it was posher than Moseley School.'

She picks a bottle of green polish from the rack and rubs it between her palms. 'I'll do your nails in their colours then. Ready for the start of term.'

To get an even coat of polish on your nails it's best to do several thin coats rather than one thick one. Any oil or grease on the nail will make the polish chip off more easily, and when it's done, you have to sit still and wait for it to dry. Moving too quick, trying to pick things up, putting your hands in your pockets, or lighting a fag will spoil it, put scars in the soft lacquer. You have to be patient, learn to meditate, take time out from the rush and bustle. Lisa tells me these things, while she tidies up. 'Watching nail polish dry is a fine art.'

She collects up a few nearly empty bottles and puts them in a bag. 'I was going to throw them away, but I thought you'd like them, for practice.'

She gives me some spare tips and a set of stencils. She tells me to have a go at doing some myself. To bring them back to her and show her how I'm getting on.

'You're a poppet,' she says, stroking my hair. I want to give her a hug. Instead I blush and look at my shoes. 'Say hello to your mum for me.'

Mum opens a packet of dried fruit.

'Prunes,' she says. 'Want one?'

'No ta.'

'C'mon, they're good for you, keep you regular.'

She only wants me to have one because she's been eating them. I take one and push it in my cheek like a hamster. I concentrate on drawing a straight silver line diagonally across my nail tip. Mum punches me on the arm, making me wobble and mess up. 'Oi, I was talking to you. Where d'you get all that stuff from? You've been visiting Lisa, haven't you? What did she tell you? Don't you listen to her. She'll tell you *anything* to get back at me.'

The trouble, she announces, is that Lisa thinks she's still a pop star. Her long nails are hideous, vulgar. 'Much better to have a tidy French polish. So much more discreet,' she informs me.

I start again with another nail and try to ignore her. She opens a packet of crisps, eats a couple and then throws the packet away. All the while she talks about Lisa, going on and on about what a waste of time she is.

'I suppose it's sad,' she says, 'at her age, not to see how ridiculous she's being.'

# 9

We should've tried it on in the shop but Mum was in such a mad rush she just grabbed it off the rails as we swooshed past. Now it's too late, I've got to be at school in half an hour and we're already miles behind.

'It doesn't fit!' she says angrily as I wiggle it up my legs. 'I can't believe it. You're too big for a size ten!'

She stands over me, yanks the skirt over my hips. I breathe in while she struggles to do it up, tearing her nail on the zip. She swears and leaves it half undone. 'I'll have to fix it with a safety pin. If you pull your shirt out over, no one'll notice.'

On the sign by the school drive – Broadhurst School for Girls – someone has scribbled out the Broad and written Slags in black marker pen. Slagshurst School for Girls. Est. 1898.

I am being marched down a corridor at high speed by the form teacher. She is talking at me too quickly, her red lipstick flashing. I can feel my skirt stretching over my hips. I hope she won't make me tuck my shirt in.

'I'm sure you'll fit in fine here, Carmen. Just remember to hold your own for the first few weeks and you'll be swimming with the swans in no time, eh?' She laughs at herself. 'I do love a little alliteration, don't you?'

Before I can answer I am projected into a classroom. A wall of faces looks up.

'Three C, this is Carmen.' She nudges me in the back. 'Say hello, Carmen.'

'Hello.' The word slips out of me like a whisper.

'This time moving your lips, please.'

There are giggles at the back of class.

'Hello,' I say again, my cheeks turning purple.

'Here you are then,' she says, her voice gone quiet like she's talking to a baby. 'You can sit next to Kelly.'

Someone giggles, a snort hidden in hands across the face. I look at Kelly: she is fat, enormous even, much much bigger than me, and her large, owl glasses with pink rims don't make her look any better. When she smiles I can see her braces, big globs of metal in her mouth.

*Osmosis.* I roll the word around my mouth. Osmosis, the way that nutrients spread through plant cells. Miss Burton draws diagrams on the board, big round circles and arrows. The density of water pushing through semi-permeable membranes. 'Permeable? You know what that means?' she asks. We shake our heads. Permeable, she says, means that you are like a sponge. It means you can absorb things. So semi-permeable means that you can absorb some things but not others. Like having a filter. It lets some things in and keeps other things out.

She shows us slides of cells under the microscope. They look like blobs of jelly.

Kelly's a Girl Guide. She tells me about it at breaktime. I can tell that she is a major square. I hang out with her because there isn't anyone else to talk to. The other girls in class don't even look at me.

Kelly takes me to the paper shop by the school gates. The man who serves us has a long, furrowed forehead, as if someone has scratched their fingers through his face to make the lines. He looks like Freddy in *Nightmare on Elm Street*, that's what I tell Kelly. I ask her if she's seen it, and she says yes, even though I bet she hasn't.

Kelly buys fistfuls of Fruit Salads and I get a Twix. We sit on the steps looking down into the playing fields. I eat my Twix slowly, chocolate first, then the caramel and finally just the biscuit, soggy where I've sucked it. Kelly puts so many Fruit Salads in her mouth she starts to drool; a long drip of spit sliding down her chin.

'Ick,' she says, wiping her face on her cardigan. 'I can't eat properly with these braces.'

Everyone's waiting outside class for registration.

'Oi you, new girl.' I look up. Two blonde girls are eyeing me like I'm a specimen in biology. 'Watcher doing with *her*? She's a lez.' They laugh.

I can't look at Kelly, I know her face is burning. I move away from her, stand on the other side of the door. The girls are laughing, saying, 'Smelly Lezzie Kelly,' over and over until the teacher walks round the corner. I push myself against the wall, pressing my shoulder blades into the over-painted sickly green, wishing they would all go away.

I'M SORRY she writes on my notebook in pencil, pressing so hard that when I rip the page out later it shows through on the other side.

WOT FOR? I write back.

She chews the end of her pencil. I'M NOT A LEZ.

NEVER SAID YOU WERE.

She tries to write an answer but I push her arm away; we're supposed to be copying off the board.

Mum is coming to get me from school. I try to get away from Kelly but I don't know where I'm going and she catches up with me.

'This way,' she says, her hand on my elbow. I shake her off. 'I'm not gonna hurt you.' She looks at me, her head cocked to one side. 'Dontcha want to come an' play PlayStation?'

She follows me to the school gates where Mum is waiting, leaning against the gateposts, smoking. 'God, I hate these places. Makes me feel fifteen again. How was it then? You making friends already?' Kelly hovers, so I have to introduce her.

'Mum, this is Kelly.'

'Pleased to meet you,' Mum says, nodding.

'Put her on a diet if she was my daughter,' Mum says once Kelly's waddled off to get the bus. She looks me up and down. I suck my stomach in.

I'm new so they're giving me time, waiting to see how I'm going to react. Paisley and Maxine. They have smooth skin, blonde highlights and boyfriends who wait for them after school. They're a bit older than me, both fifteen. They think they are sophisticated. We're waiting in the queue for lunch.

'Hey, Carmen, what kind of name is that?'

'Spanish,' I say. 'My dad comes from Barcelona.'

'Are you mental?' Paisley asks. Maxine snorts and bites her lip.

'No.'

81

'Well, people will think you are if you hang out with Kelly. She's *retarded*.'

'You wanna sit with us? Can if you like.' Maxine is being generous. I am expected to be grateful.

'Thanks,' I say.

Paisley has salad so I pick a salad too and a Diet Coke.

Maxine unpacks a Tupperware box from her backpack. Her Tupperware box is full of smaller Tupperware boxes. 'I'm on Weight Watchers,' she says, 'One protein, two carbohydrates, and one treat.' She shows us a tuna salad, two wheat crackers and a Milky Way.

'We watch what we eat,' Paisley says, fluttering her mascaraed eyes at me. She is the leader because she is the prettiest. She nibbles on a lettuce leaf to prove her point. 'Too much saturated fat in chips. Gives you spots.'

I bring my hand to my face without thinking. There is a big angry zit developing on my chin.

'Like your nails,' Paisley says, holding my fingers. 'They're *way* cool.' Her eyes widen, I can tell she's impressed.

'Thanks,' I say, 'my aunt's a technician.' I push my salad away. 'I'm not hungry.'

Paisley makes a face. 'Me neither, the food here's, like, *totally* disgusting.'

'Look, it's Kelly.' Maxine points to the till, where Kelly is paying for her dinner. 'State of her.' She curls her lip.

'Hey lez,' they say, loud enough for her to hear as she walks past. 'Kelly belly.'

Kelly looks over, eyes magnified by her lenses. I stick my tongue out; she flinches and looks away.

Maxine has a copy of *Vogue*, stolen off her mum. The pages are crumpled and sticky, the cover curling at the edges.

'Paisley's going to be a model,' she says. 'Aren't you, Paisley?'

Paisley flicks her long highlighted hair and smiles slowly.

I smile at her. 'You've got good hair,' I say.

'Thanks.' She touches her fringe self-consciously.

I decide that being friends with Paisley will be easy. All she wants is an audience.

I get the bus from school on my own. I eat a bag of cola cubes, crunching them until my teeth hurt. At the back someone's smoking weed; the thick smell drifts down the aisle, sweeter than cigarettes.

It's sunny, with big cartoon clouds and the trees are just starting to turn. I finish the cola cubes and lick my teeth to get all the flavour off.

I get off in town and go to Burger King on the way home. I get a Whopper and a chocolate milkshake and eat them really quickly as I walk down the street, keeping an eye out in case Mum is in the crowds of shoppers. I stand outside the flat, wiping ketchup off my lips with my sleeve and suck a Polo in case she smells it.

But when I get in she's not even there.

# 10

We're doing photosynthesis. Looking at geranium leaves. Light turning to energy. Kelly is sucking pear drops that make her smell like nail polish. Her braces make her lips stick out and she snuffles when she sucks, breathing loudly through her nose like she's mental or something.

I give her a spider nip on the leg. She squeaks and dribbles on her exercise book.

'Whaddya do that for?' she whispers. 'I haven't done nothing.'

She looks pathetic. '*Lezzie*,' I hiss. 'Lezzie Kelly.'

She shifts away from me, hiding her book with her arm. 'Piss off,' she says.

After class we wait for her: me, Paisley and Maxine.

'Hey Kelly,' Paisley puts her arm out to stop her from passing. 'We think you should apologize.'

'Wha'?'

I wish she'd shut her mouth. Her braces make me feel ill.

'Yeah, lezzie, say sorry.' Maxine stands close to her, her breasts pushed forward.

'I haven't done nothing.' Tears begin to wet the corners of her eyes. 'Whadd've I done?'

'You're fat,' I say. 'And you're ugly.' I can see the whites of her eyes, glossy, like boiled eggs. Apologize.'

'I'm sorry.' She's really crying now.

I suck in my cheeks, pool saliva in my mouth and spit it at her. Strings of white soak into her cardigan.

Paisley tugs my arm. 'Teacher,' she hisses in my ear. 'Teacher.'

We pull back, flatten ourselves against the corridor. Kelly waddles off. 'I'm gonna get you, smelly,' I whisper at her back. Paisley giggles.

'You're mad you are, Carmen. You wanna come to my party? We're going uptown on Saturday to get outfits.'

'*Paisley*,' Maxine nudges her and makes a face.

''S all right, Carmen doesn't mind if we've got boyfriends, do you? You got a boyfriend, Carmen?'

'I had one before, where I lived,' I lie.

Paisley makes a face, 'Aww, ju miss him? I miss Carter. Wanna see a picture?' She gets her purse out of her bag and flips it open to show me the photo inside. 'Isn't he adorable?' It's a blurry picture of a man on a beach. 'That was when he was in Ibiza. He's a DJ.'

'Gorgeous,' I say, though he could be deformed for all I can see.

'She's going out with his best mate,' Paisley nudges Maxine. ''Nat right, Maxine?'

Maxine looks at me sulkily. I don't think she really likes me, I think she wants to be Paisley's best friend.


They're waiting for me outside HMV. Mum's given me a tenner and told me not to get lost. 'Come to the shop if you don't know where you are.' I've got my tracksuit on, my Adidas trainers and the Nike baseball cap that Dad bought me for Christmas. Mum moaned when she saw me in it, she said I should make more of an effort if I'm trying to make new friends.

'Hi-ya,' they wave at me from across the street.

It's cold, the sky a concrete grey. Maxine has dyed her hair. It's supposed to be blonde but in the glare of the shop lights it looks a bit green.

'Whatcher think?' she asks, tugging at a strand. 'Did it myself. You should get streaks done, you know, Carmen. I can do it for you, my sister's a hairdresser.'

Paisley is smoking a fag, puffing it out really fast like she's blowing away dust. 'Wanna fag?'

'No ta.'

We walk around the split levels of HMV looking at the CDs. Paisley's into boy bands. She runs her fingers over the cellophane casing.

'Look at his muscles,' she says.

'Oh no, he's *vile*,' Maxine says, pointing to another one with a thick face and a little goatee beard. 'He's the one I like.'

They all have brown skin and white teeth and earrings in their ears.

'What kind of music you into, Carmen?'

I look at the wall of CDs. Madonna pouts out at me. I point to her.

Maxine makes a face. 'She's so old.'

'Look, it's Kelly,' Paisley says, pointing to a picture of Mr Greedy on a T-shirt. We laugh.

'C'mon, let's look in Top Shop.'

We walk down the street arm in arm, Paisley in the middle. Maxine keeps giving me snidey looks, until I have to pull my cap down to shade my eyes from her gaze.

Top Shop is heaving. Maxine elbows a couple of ten-year-olds out the way to get to the clothes on the New Season rail. She picks out a T-shirt made out of glittery material that looks like it should fit a Barbie doll, and holds it up to herself.

'Whaddya reckon?'

Paisley turns up her nose. ''S a bit cheap looking. What about this one?' She picks out a furry leopardskin jacket.

'*Paisley*, I'm not going in that, it looks like something my nan would wear.'

'Who's going to be there?' I ask.

'Oh, everybody,' Paisley says, flicking her hair. 'It's gonna be *wild*.'

We go to the changing rooms together.

'Aren't you going to get anything, Carmen?' Maxine asks. 'Sportswear's a bit *out* now.'

'No it isn't,' Paisley says, 'it was everywhere at the Clothes Show. Madonna wears them trainers.'

Maxine makes a face. She can't contradict Paisley because she's more beautiful than her.

The fitting rooms are small cubicles, two rows, facing each other, with thin orange curtains for privacy. We huddle together in one at the end.

'Shut the curtain will ya,' Maxine says, elbowing past me and yanking the curtain. It rips off its hooks.

'*Maxine*, you broke it,' Paisley whispers, giggling.

'Oh, sort it will you, Carmen?'

She gives me the ripped end and I hold it up to try and cover the gap.

I can see into the cubicle opposite. The woman hasn't even bothered shutting the curtain. She's got bright blue streaks in her hair and black clothes, and she's taking off a leather jacket. *Distress '79 – Out of Control* it says on the back in faded white paint. Her arms are thick as hams and covered with tattoos. A thin T-shirt clings to her figure, showing up all the places where her body bulges. She's got a leather choker round her neck and her tight skirt exaggerates the curves of her bum. Her boots are high, snakeskin and pointed at the toes.

I catch her eye in the mirror but she doesn't seem to see me, it's more like she's looking through me. She has dark make-up round her eyes, earrings, blue lipstick that glistens in the harsh light.

She starts to take off her top, showing me her back, her bra strap, the tattoos on her shoulder blades, the way that her skin folds and ripples. I realize I have let the curtain hang open.

'Shut the bloody curtain, Carmen,' Maxine says, loudly. 'There's a freak out there.'

She runs a hand over a belly that is flat and taut, smooth as a ski slope. She makes a face at the mirror.

'I'm fat,' she says.

'Don't be stupid,' Paisley says. She has a pair of jeans to try on even though she says she can't afford anything.

Maxine puts on the glittery T-shirt. 'Don't look cheap on,' she says. Then quickly, before anyone sees, she puts her old top over it and then her jacket.

'C'mon,' she says, 'let's go.'

Paisley has got one leg into the jeans. 'Wait for us outside, Maxie?'

Maxine looks at me. 'C'mon then, Carmen.' She links arms with me when I stand up and makes me stride out of the changing rooms. The woman opposite has gone.

'She was a right lezzer,' she says, sneering.

Maxine gives the assistant a tag for four – but only three items of clothes. Then we're walking so fast we're nearly running. She squashes into me, like we're best mates. 'Just talk to me,' she hisses. I don't know what to say, my heart's pounding. We go past the security and I expect the alarm to go off but it doesn't. I wonder how she got the tag off, I never saw her do it.

We stand up the road a bit, outside Boots, watching for Paisley. Maxine bites her lip.

'Come on, come on, hurry up.'

She lights a fag and coughs. The damp air makes my nipples stick out, hard and sore.

While we're waiting the woman with blue hair comes out of the shop and up the road towards us.

Maxine giggles and sings the theme tune to the *Addams Family*.

The woman's heels click on the pavement, hips swinging inside her skirt. When she gets level with us, she looks Maxine straight in the eye, her red lips stuck together in a little smile as if she's going to give her a kiss. But she sticks her tongue out instead, showing us a silver stud in the middle of it. Maxine looks frightened for a moment, then pissed off.

'Bitch!' Maxine says, but only when the woman's moved past us. I watch her heels, her legs moving with the same deliberate, steady rhythm up the street.

When Paisley joins us, Maxine is full of it.

'Should be locked up,' she says. 'People like that. She was a right perv, wasn't she, Carmen?'

'You'll get over it,' I say, which makes Paisley laugh.

'Yeah, serves you right, Maxie, you shouldda waited for us.'

'Oh, piss off.' She looks really cross now, her mouth turning down meanly at the edges. I give the finger to her back as we walk up New Street to Pret A Manger for lunch.

'Ugh, what is it?' I look at the rolled up bits of flesh and blobs of rice.

'Sushi,' Paisley says. 'Japanese, innit? Raw fish.'

'Looks weird,' I say.

''S good for ya, got no calories in it. You should try it.'

'Go on,' Maxine holds a box out to me. 'You'll like it.'

It's really expensive, but I get one anyway. We sit in the window with our sushi. Paisley and Maxine pick at it, eating tiny scraps of food.

'What's in it?' I ask as I open the box.

'Seaweed, prawns, soy sauce.'

'Seaweed?' I think of all the slimy fingers of bladderwrack at the seaside and want to puke. 'I can't eat that.'

''S got no calories in it.'


The boys are meeting us by the cathedral in Pigeon Park. We sit on one of the tombstones, on a plastic bag to protect us from the bird shit. Paisley fixes her make-up in her compact mirror, Maxine lights a fag.

'Witches' tits,' she says, shivering. 'It's *freezing* out here.'

The cold pinches at our faces; it makes Paisley look really skinny, highlighting her cheekbones. 'There they are,' she says pointing at two figures walking up an alleyway by the City Plaza, their trainers a dazzling white. 'Pretend like you haven't see them,' she says, turning primly to face the other way.

I watch the swirl of people in front of us, coats and leaves flying in the stiffening breeze, making us shiver. I count to ten and they still haven't come up behind us. Paisley makes it to twenty before she turns round.

'Hey? Where've they gone?'

'Mebbe they never saw us.'

'What the—'

Suddenly they're on us, roaring and shrieking and tickling Paisley and Maxine. They nearly knock me on the floor.

'Oooh, you bastards,' Paisley says.

Carter has big red spots and a gold earring; Dean has blue splodgy tattoos on his wrists. They look older than eighteen.

'Who's this then?' Carter asks, pointing at me.

'Carmen. She's new.'

'Please t'meet you,' he says, sitting down and pulling Paisley on to his lap by her hips. Dean and Maxine are already snogging; she is straddling him and sticking her tongue right in his mouth.


'C'mon,' Carter says, 'let's go back to mine.'

Paisley gets up and grabs my arm. 'You coming?' she says, as if I was about to leave. 'C'mon, he's got Jack Daniels and everything.'

Carter's got an old brown Fiesta, parked on the double yellows round the back of the library. It's got big rust stains up the side and a Magic Tree air freshener hanging off the rear-view mirror.

'It's the *Turdis*,' Carter says in a silly voice. 'If it looks like shit and goes like shit, then it *is* shit.'

He gives it some on the expressway out of town though. The chassis starts to rattle and the engine makes a strained, whining noise.

Dean and Maxine whoop, but Paisley's scared, she asks him to slow down. I watch Birmingham flashing past so quickly it turns to a blur, a rush of houses and people.

I press my cheek against the glass and wish that I were back in Yorkshire.

Carter's flat is in a road of houses, opposite a tall warehouse. The warehouse is so big I have to hold my breath when I look up. Rubbish spills into the road out the front of Carter's flat; there's a shopping trolley and an old bike frame half buried in the long grass.

Inside, the lounge is bare apart from a sofa, a TV, a stereo and a withered pot plant on the window ledge. A postcard of Bob Marley is stuck on the wall with curling sticky tape. Dean has made a joint and he's passing it round, Maxine's nearly choking herself trying to smoke it. Paisley's slugging on the bottle of JD, wincing every time she swallows.

'School's wank, isn't it?' Paisley sighs, flicking her hair. 'I'm gonna leave when I get a modelling job. Get a private tutor.'

'I'll teach you a thing or two.' Carter tickles her and she squeals really loudly.

'Here, Carmen.' Maxine passes me the spliff. I take a few pulls and pass it on. I can feel myself getting dizzy from the nicotine. I put my hands under my armpits to keep them warm.

'It's freezing,' I say.

'God! She talks,' Carter says, jumping. 'I was beginning to wonder what you sounded like, babe. I thought you were going to sit there all night like one of them sphinxes.'

I smile, but I don't say anything. Keeping quiet weirds people out; it makes them paranoid, it makes them think that you're thinking about them.

Maxine shows off her robbed top, telling the boys how she nicked it. She flashes her belly button and her silky

92

white bra at us while she talks, holding the centre of attention. They look impressed and start telling us a story about how they swagged four bottles of Jack Daniels between them from Safeway in Kings Heath.

'Stuck 'em down me trousers,' Dean says, grinning.

Carter gets a bag of grass out of his pocket and starts to skin up on his knees. 'Someone put some tunes on.'

When the joint's gone round, Dean and Maxine start really going for it, almost doing it in front of us on the couch. Maxine's got her mouth open so wide she looks like she's going to be sick.

'Hey, you two, wanna use the bedroom?' Carter taps Dean on the shoulder.

He looks up at us and grins. 'Yeah, right, sorry, c'mon, babes.' He squeezes the flesh of Maxine's arse.

We can hear them doing it over the music. Maxine makes little squeaking noises, Dean grunts loudly. I try to ignore it, focusing instead on the warm, stoned feeling I got from the joint, but Carter starts laughing.

'It's disgusting,' he says, grinning. He starts making exaggerated humping noises. 'Oh, oh, oh, oh, oh, yes, yes, yes, oh, baby.'

Paisley moves ever so slightly away from him. 'We've gotta go soon. Right, Carmen?'

'Whenever,' I shrug.

This is obviously not what she wanted me to say and she pulls a face at me. Carter's hand is creeping up her leg, pushing between her thighs. She gets up.

'C'mon,' she says, grabbing her bag. 'Mum'll kill me if I'm not in by six.'

'Hang on,' Carter says. 'Aren't yous gonna wait for Maxine? I'll give ya a lift back uptown.'

The noise from the other room has stopped.

'Nah,' she says, 'C'mon, Carmen.' She grabs my arm. 'Let's go.' She pushes me out of the door in front of her. 'See ya at the party, Carter.'

On the way to the bus stop we pass a chippie.

'You hungry, Carmen?' Paisley asks, looking at me slyly out of the corner of her eye. I can feel my stomach cramping with hunger.

'Nah,' I say.

She pauses. 'Me neither.'

# 11

Mum is polishing an apple on her skirt like a cricket ball. She holds it to her mouth and rubs the shiny surface over her lips. She sniffs it and licks it and bites it a tiny bit, chewing off a fleck of skin.

'Can I stop over at Paisley's on Saturday?' I ask.

'Who's Paisley?'

'Friend from school.'

'The lard bucket?' She takes another nibble of her apple. Her eyes are fixed on the TV.

'No, that's Kelly. Paisley's the one I went to town with.'

'Where does she live?'

'Kings Heath.'

'What you going for?'

'A party.'

'Will her parents be there?'

'Think so,' I say.

'All right. But I want her address and phone number. I don't want you going missing so I don't know where to find you.'

She puts the apple in her mouth almost whole, like she could eat it all in one go, then she spits it out again, and takes another, tiny nibble. I look at her ears; I can see little pinprick scars where she used to have rings in.

'Can I get my ears pierced?' I ask.

She puts her hand to her ear, then smiles. 'You can spend your money on what you like, long as it isn't food.' She looks at me benevolently. 'What you going to wear?'

She gets out her catalogues from work. The ring binders with all the latest designs. Apparently, women in Birmingham like a brassier kind of look than the women in Yorkshire.

'See that shift dress?' she says pointing at a model wearing a flimsy powder blue, nightie-type thing. 'Now your average Londoner bought those by the vanload. They couldn't get to them fast enough. It's the kind of fabric that makes most women feel glamorous, but not too tarty, kind of sophisticated. But I didn't sell one in the shop back home. Not one—'

She breaks off, stares into space.

'Why?' I prompt.

'Women up north like to call a spade a spade. No pretensions. They know what suits them, they wouldn't be seen dead in stuff like this.' She taps the page with her fingers. 'Make you look like a sack of potatoes unless you're Claudia Schiffer.'

'Oh.'

'Now here,' she points to an embroidered black dress with a similar cut. 'This covers all your sins. Little black number. You can hide all your lumps and bumps under one of those and no one will notice. Sold more of those than I've had hot dinners, even with all that hippie trim.' She pauses, chewing on a bit of apple. 'What d'you reckon?'

I look more closely at the photograph; the dress has a kind of Red Indian theme, with feather tassels at the waist and orange embroidery round the hem. I shrug.

''S all right.'

'Well I think you'd look just perfect in it. You're getting old enough for party frocks now.' She sighs. 'Really, you're so lucky, whole world ahead of you. If I had my time again I'd, well—' she stops, scrapes another fleck off the apple with her teeth. 'No knowing what I could have done.'

# 12

The Sea Life Centre is a round grey building right by the canal, opposite the Indoor Arena where they film *Gladiators*. As part of a publicity drive Miss Burton got free tickets and glossy souvenir programmes from the company that runs the Centre.

'*Told* you it was crap,' Maxine says as we go through the doors and look up the landscaped slope of tanks and waterfalls and fake rocks. She's been here before with her family. '*Gladiators* was miles better.'

Paisley nudges her. 'Maxine, I was into that when I was, like, *eight*.'

Maxine blushes and turns away from us. She gives Paisley the finger in a way that makes it obvious that she isn't being funny. She's still pissed off with us for leaving her in Carter's flat. 'You couldda *waited* for me. We'd nearly *finished*.'

There's a Captain Pugwash theme to all the displays, obviously intended for much younger kids. Miss Burton leads the way, explaining about lifecycles and habitats. We straggle behind, taking the piss, Paisley making jokes about Seaman Stains and Little Willy.

'It *smells* in here, Miss,' Paisley says.

'Yeah, tell Kelly to put some deodorant on, Miss,'

Maxine says, quietly, but still loud enough for Kelly to hear.

In one room there's a tank with two blue catfish. They are like cats that have been turned into fish: round, cartoon-cat faces and whiskers and soft, flabby bodies that settle about them as they wiggle on the bottom. I fold my arms across my chest, try to push my breasts back in.

'They look like Kelly,' Maxine says, giggling. 'Where is Belly? Hey, Kelly, look over here, it's you. *Belly's gonna get you, Belly's gonna get you,*' she chants. But Kelly is ignoring her, walking close to Miss Burton for safety.

Next to the catfish, mackerel shoal in a circular tank, round and round and round, making me dizzy. They are silvery and streamlined, designed for speed, for zipping across thousands of miles of ocean. Their eyes shine balefully as they swim past.

'Doncha think it's cruel? Keeping them in like that,' I say.

'Naah,' Paisley says. 'This place is well into conservation, it says so.' She points to the souvenir programme.

We're mooching behind everyone else. When we try to go in to the Digital Domain, Miss Burton shoos us out. 'You're late,' she says. 'You'll have to miss the film, I'm not having you spoiling it for everyone else.'

Maxine starts to moan, but Miss Burton shuts the door on us. ''S crap anyway, c'mon let's go and have a fag on the balcony.'

She goes off with Paisley, and I stay behind to look at the rockpool display. In one tank, all by itself, is a hermit crab, right up close to the edge of the tank, propping itself up on a huge pair of claws.

The programme says that hermit crabs are shy, that they steal shells from other molluscs because their bodies are too soft to grow their own. A diagram shows what one looks like without its shell: a shapeless sac of membranes and organs.

I hold my nails up to the glass and wave my fingers. The crab has eyes that stick out on stalks. They twitch and follow the movement of my hand. Then suddenly, as if startled, it scuttles sideways across the gravel, towards the fake rockery at the back of the tank, withdrawing into its shell so only the tips of its claws are showing.

The toilets at the entrance to the Titanic Adventure have doors done up like airlocks with wheels on them and metallic paint. Maxine nudges us. 'Kelly's just gone in there. C'mon.'

Miss Burton's not looking, she's listening to the guide, her hands clasped in front of her legs, head cocked to one side. The guide is reading from a script about the Titanic and the amazing fishtank downstairs, where we will get to walk underneath the water.

Kelly's the only one in the toilets. Paisley knocks on the door of her cubicle. 'C'mon, Kelly, we're bursting.'

'Yeah, let us in Belly.'

'Go *away*.'

Maxine stands on the toilet of the adjacent cubicle and looks over the top.

'Oi,' she says, 'you're not doing anything. Why aren't you doing anything? You should be having a piss if you're sitting on the bog.'

She jumps down off the toilet. 'She's not doing anything,' she says again.

She kicks the cubicle door. It flies open, hitting Kelly with a crack and bouncing back with a slam.

Paisley steps back.

There's silence for a moment then Kelly wails pathetically. 'You *broke* them.'

When Maxine pushes the door open Kelly's sitting there with her knickers round her knees, holding her glasses. One of the lenses is split in half.

'Poor Belly,' Maxine says.

'Smelly,' says Paisley.

'Lezzie.'


We go down in the lift, a breathy woman's voice telling us to get out at the third level. The doors open and we are staring at the bottom of a huge tank with a tunnel underneath it. Miss Burton is in the middle, pointing out something to swotty Sally Jenks who's taking notes.

Rays and sharks and sea bass swim towards us, fins undulating, almost in slow motion.

'Wow,' Paisley says. 'It's not crap.'

'Miss, what would happen if this collapsed. Would we die?' Maxine shouts.

'If there's any justice in this world, Maxine, yes,' Miss Burton mutters.

One of the rays has lost part of its tail, and there's a sea bass lying on the bottom, not moving. I wonder why nobody else has noticed and nudge Paisley.

'Gro-*oss*,' she says.

The displays lead out into the gift shop and the café. Miss Burton gives us questionnaires and tells us that if we fill them in we'll get a free keyring. Paisley spends loads on a seahorse pen and a notebook.

We sit in the café drinking mineral water.

'I don't want a poxy keyring,' Maxine says, writing *crap* as her answers to all the questions.

'The seahorses were beautiful,' Paisley says, using her new seahorse pen.

I write hermit crab for all the answers except the question about the things that I would change. PUT THEM ALL BACK, I write.

Maxine opens up a copy of *Marie Claire*. We flick through it, tracing our fingers across the shiny pages of models and clothes and celebrities. Everybody's thin and glamorous.

'God, she looks a state,' Maxine says pointing to some picture of a Hollywood starlet.

'I want a pair of those,' Paisley says, as she turns the page. 'I love shoes like that.' She points to a pair of cowboy boots.

'Ewww, Paisley. Greasy rockers wear stuff like that.'

'Watcher gonna wear to the party then, Carmen?'

They both look at me expectantly. I shrug. 'Surprise,' I say.

I eat the bag of chips too quickly. They're boiling, just out of the fryer, and they scald me inside as they go down. I hang round at the bottom of the tower block, keeping an eye out for Mum. When I'm finished, I kick the wrappers under a parked car.

I change into my tracksuit and lie on my bed. The chips sit in a heavy clump on my stomach. I run my hands over my belly and worry about what I'm going to wear to the party. Mum has left a copy of *Elle* on my bed. She thinks if I read the magazines I will learn how to be ladylike. Never a real lady, only like one. I let it slide to the floor, the heavy slick of pages slumping against the side of the divan.

The traffic sounds like the sea, the constant *swoosh swoosh* as it surges around the ring road. I dream that I am lying on a beach, except I'm not inside myself at all. I'm looking down at my body from the sky. I think I must be a bird, maybe a seagull. My skin is filmy, almost transparent; I can see my heart, my lungs, my bones. The sun pulses, hotter and hotter; I'm getting redder, slowly starting to burn. I try to hover above myself, spreading my wings as far as they will go, to keep the sun off with my shadow.

Then I realize that I'm not above my body at all, that this was the dream. I'm stranded. The tide has gone out, further than the horizon, and the beach has turned into desert. I try to move my arms but when I look, my hands have turned to huge claws, sunk into the sand, too heavy to lift. My tongue is swollen and dry in my mouth. I can't move, I can't breathe. I'm washed up, my body a thin membrane sac with no shell, shrivelling on the sharp sand.

Mum turns the light on.

'C'mon, lazy. Supper.'

I feel sick when I sit up; my mouth dried to nothing. It's nearly ten o clock. Mum said she had the deliveries to deal with at work.

We sit in front of the telly, the LoFat Micro Food on our knees. Mine's supposed to be lasagne but it's gone all melted in the microwave and looks like sludge. I eat it really quick so I don't have to taste it.

'Sweetheart, what have I told you about eating slowly? You'll never lose weight if you gobble like that. And it's really unattractive, look – you've got it all round your mouth.'

I wipe my mouth with my sleeve.

She sighs and talks to me really slowly, like I'm a baby or something. 'Honey, I want you to do something for me, OK?'

'What?'

'I want you to keep a little diary, like we did before, remember? Write down for me everything that you eat. I mean everything. OK?'

'Why?'

She pushes her tray of food away from her, virtually untouched.

'How old are you now, Carmen?'

'Fourteen.'

'Exactly. Old enough to learn about make-up and clothes. God knows you've been wearing sportswear since you were a toddler. Don't you think it's time you changed your image? Just a little bit?' She pinches her fingers together. 'If you lost weight, you'd look lovely in some of our petite range.' She looks at me pleadingly, her eyes like planets. 'No more Big Macs on the way home from school? You think I don't know about these things, Carmen, but I do. *I do.*'

She gets up, taking our trays into the kitchen. She's hardly made an impression on her dinner.

# 13

Mum's working all day on Saturday. 'The shops don't stop,' she says, giving me some money for the bus. Outside, gangs of men in fluorescent overalls are digging up the road. All the bus stops have moved further up into town. I walk up the hill towards the station. *It's Time For A Change* says a banner on the inside of the Rotunda windows. I look at a picture on a hoarding showing what the new Bull Ring will be like when they've finished the redevelopment. An artist's impression of model people strolling in the sunshine, sitting outside the new glass-fronted café-bars.

The wind sweeps down Queensway, making me shiver in my thin tracksuit top. I pull my baseball cap down over my forehead. Mum says she's going to burn it. She says it's giving me spots.

Signs at the entrance to the Bull Ring markets read: *Countdown to Closing. Making a Better Birmingham.* On bright yellow paper, like a warning. Inside, some of the stalls aren't even open. In Stitches is closed, the shutters down, the lights off.

Lisa is serving a woman with long, curly nails. She's having them done pink with little rings and jewels. She's got short hair dyed to look like leopardskin, and tattoos.

'All right, sunshine,' Lisa says, not looking up. 'I was hoping you'd come and visit.'

Leopardskin woman gives me a funny look and whistles through her teeth.

'You weren't wrong, Lisa, she's the living image.' She looks at me. 'Your mum still living the champagne life-style? She still dissing us? Don't expect you recognize me, do you? I had more hair in them days.' She smiles, showing a glittering gold tooth. 'Annmarie,' she says, 'pleased t' meet ya.'

'Who's the living image?' I ask.

'Never you mind,' Lisa says, arching a narrow eyebrow at Annmarie. 'What you doing here? Where's your mam?'

'Working,' I say, 'I'm supposed to be going to Nana's but they've moved all the bus stops.'

Annmarie sighs. 'Tell me about it. You can't move for builders' cracks round here nowadays.' Lisa giggles. 'It's a crying shame. Where are we all going to go?'

Lisa looks at Annmarie. 'We'll find somewhere,' she says. 'People like us always do.'

I hop from foot to foot, unsure if I should stay or go. Lisa puts Annmarie's hands under a lamp to dry her nails.

'You tell me if that gets too hot. You want a cup of tea, Carmen? Come round here, love.'

She opens a little door, just wide enough to squeeze through. Inside it's like a tiny caravan but made even smaller by the shelves that glitter with their rainbow of polish bottles. She pulls a stool out for me.

'You sit down there. Hardly enough room to breathe is there? Especially with my fat backside in the way.' She rubs her hands across her bum. 'Still, I suppose it's useful to grow cushions if you're sitting down all day.' She picks up my hands, inspects my nails. 'Hmm,' she says, 'could do with a bit of a trim. What colour d'you like?'

I look at Annmarie, engrossed in a magazine.

'I'm going to a party,' I say, trying to whisper. 'I don't know what I'm going to wear.'

She stops for a second and looks at me, her mouth forming an O. 'Haven't you talked to your mum about this?' she asks.

I make a face. 'I don't like her clothes,' I say.

The kettle boils, steam billowing into the booth. It doesn't switch off, just keeps on boiling, water splashing out of the spout. Lisa pulls the plug out of the wall. 'Taint what you wear, it's the way that you wear it, you know.'

'*Bollocks*,' Annmarie says. 'I think I chipped it.'

Lisa tuts and grabs her nail file. 'I told you to sit still.'

'Oooh, don't say that, I'm all pins today. 'Swat you get for getting older . . .' she shivers. 'Shit for nerves.'

Lisa gives her a stern look. 'And all those late nights. They catch up on you in the end.'

'You haven't got nothing to wear, eh?' Annmarie winks. 'Don't believe a word of it. You're just bored with your wardrobe. Believe me, I know the feeling, sweetheart, it happens to me every time I open mine.' She says if I wait for her nails she'll take me to Patti's stall in the Rag.

Lisa says she'll come with us. 'Because you'll come back wrapped in Bacofoil if I don't.'

When Annmarie's nails have dried she pays Lisa and shrugs herself into a pink mac. It's a leather the same colour as her nails, trimmed with pink marabou cuffs.

'I like your mac,' I say.

'Superfly isn't it?' She drops a little curtsey. 'See, Lees? Carmen likes my clothes.'

'Oh shush, you old slapper.'

'Old slapper! Get her.'

They go on like this all the way down past St Martin's to the Rag Market. Me in between them, like a hostage.

The Rag Market is across the road from the Bull Ring. Next to the spiky Gothic of St Martin's Church which has gone a sooty black from all the pollution.

The Rag is like a giant aircraft hangar, made from corrugated metal. It is packed full of stalls. Mostly clothes, materials, shoes, soft furnishings, though there are other stalls too, selling bric-a-brac, records, books, kitchen stuff, incense. Patti's stall is in the middle, partitioned off with bright lime-green curtains. She makes her own clubwear: velvet trousers, see-through T-shirts, rubber tops, sequin thongs, animal print jackets.

She's tall with bleached blonde hair that straggles over her shoulders. She's wearing a black velvet hat, pulled down on one side over her ear.

'Watcher,' she says, when she sees us. 'You been kid-napping children again?'

Lisa laughs. 'This is Carmen.'

Patti winks at me. 'I've heard so *much* about you.'

Annmarie shows off her nails while Lisa picks out some T-shirts, and a blue apron top that looks like it's made from sparkly sandpaper. 'How about this one' – she offers it to me – 'with a good pair of jeans?'

'You'll need a decent bra with that mind,' Annmarie says. 'Something to give you a bit of, you know, *lift*.' She grabs a tape measure and runs it round my chest. 'You hang on a sec. I'll go and get you one.'

She comes back with a black padded bra hanging off one of her fingernails. 'Go on, put this on underneath.'

They push me into Patti's changing room which is just

a shower curtain that draws round in a circle. You have to clip it together with pegs to keep it shut. There's no hooks or anything, and I have to drop my clothes on the floor. I can see their shoes through the gap at the bottom of the curtain: Lisa's red slingbacks, Annmarie's leopard-skin boots, Patti's shiny PVC shoes with thick rubber soles.

'Mirror's out here, love. C'mon out, don't be shy, let's have a look at you.'

I pull back the curtain tentatively, half hiding behind it.

They all look at me and smile. Patti's grinning.

'Well, there's pretty,' she says.

'As a picture,' says Lisa.

Annmarie grabs me by the shoulders and turns me towards the mirror. 'Isn't that gorgeous?'

The light makes the glittery top shimmer. The curve of my chest is voluptuous, grown up even. I look like I could be in a magazine.

'*Wicked*,' I say. I hardly dare breathe.

'Just you wait,' Lisa says. 'We've only just started.'

There are two girls wanting an appointment waiting outside the Nail File.

'Sorry,' Lisa says, pushing me past them. 'Won't be free for another hour.'

Annmarie insists that I put my hair up in knots. She shows me how, twisting a clump of my hair into little coils on my head. I like it, so they carry on: Lisa twists it up and Annmarie puts blue glitter all along my hairline.

'Ooooh,' Annmarie giggles. 'It's just like having a Girl's World.'

When they're done with my hair, Lisa holds up some temporary tattoos. 'One of these would be cool.'

I let her put a vicious-looking crab on my shoulder and a Celtic band on my arm.

They stand back and make me do a twirl. Now there's only my nails left to do.

'Wish I was going to this party,' Annmarie mutters.

I admire myself in the mirror, while they tweak my hair and brush glitter off my trousers. 'You'll knock 'em dead.'

'Better go,' Annmarie says, collecting her bags. 'Off to sprinkle my fairy dust somewhere else. Ta-ra-a-bit.' She kisses Lisa on both cheeks and me on my forehead.

Strutting through the shoppers, her pink shape makes a sharp outline against the greeny-grey of the market crowd.

'She's a diamond,' Lisa says as we watch her disappear up the escalator. 'Talk you to tears, mind, if you let her.'

Lisa does my nails red-and-blue stripes with silvery number eights in the middle of each one.

'What's going to happen to the markets?' I ask her as she paints the blue stripes on.

'Who knows?' She shrugs. 'They're building new ones. It's all coming down, the Bull Ring, the Rag. But the new rents will be more expensive. There's lots of us moving on. Like the diaspora, it is. Everyone's getting out of town. There's a few stopping, but there won't be as much room as before and it won't be the same atmosphere.'

'It's a shame,' I say.

'Crying shame if you ask me. I mean, we all want it different. Don't get me wrong. No one wants to work in a scuzz hole like this, but when you look at the plans it just seems a bit, well, posh. There—' she finishes the final number eight with a flourish. 'You look like a right little star in that outfit. Finished off with basketball nails by Lisa. You tell people if they ask that it was me that did them.'

On the bus up to Nana's I tap them against the window, the nails dancing like little cheerleaders up and down the plastic glass.

Nana's watching UK Gold. *Bergerac* and *Knots Landing*.

'Don't remember it, do you?' she says to me. 'Telly was good in those days.'

She doesn't even notice that I'm late.

The living room is gloomy. Grandad's hedge has grown even bigger, almost as high as the guttering. Outside the window is a dense wall of green.

'Can I put the light on?' I ask.

'You can do what you like, love,' she says, not moving from her seat. 'I've bought some chocolate biscuits and some crisps, they're on the side in the kitchen.'

She's bought Wagon Wheels, Tunnock's Marshmallow Teacakes and Hula Hoops.

'Oooh, give us one of those teacakes.'

I sink my teeth into the chocolate and marshmallow.

'Have another, have another,' she says when she sees that I've only eaten one. 'I bought them for you, they'll only go to waste.'

But when I ignore her, she eats them herself and when she's finished with the teacakes she makes a start on the Wagon Wheels, eating each one in nearly a whole bite.

I sit really gingerly in the chair. Lisa told me to be careful not to smudge myself. I put my elbows on my knees, prop my head in my hands. My hair feels like it might fall out any minute.

I flick through Nana's *Woman's Realm*. Fashion for the

over fifties, amazing stories of bravery and courage and exotic meals in minutes. The cookery pages are sticky and greasy. I have to rip some of them to get them open.

In the advert breaks I check my reflection in Nana's bathroom mirror.

'You got problems downstairs?' she asks, when I get up for the fourth time in an hour. I flash my nails, hoping she'll notice, but she's already gone back to the TV. 'Have a Wagon Wheel, love.'

'I don't want a bloody Wagon Wheel,' I say, but under my breath so she can't hear. I hate her: fat cow. She's trying to make me fat like her, just like she did with Mum.

Her bathroom suite is a sludgy-green plastic. There's dark stains on the carpet around the toilet and bits everywhere: novelty soaps, plastic ducks, a Welsh lady toilet-roll holder, candlesticks, backscrubbers and, tucked down the back of the radiator, an old copy of Grandad's *Racing Post*. Everything's jumbled up, messy.

I pull poses for the mirror, watch myself sparkle as the glitter catches the light; tiny constellations twinkling in my hair.

'*Wicked*,' I whisper. '*Wicked*.'


'Where on God's *earth* did you get that?' she asks when she sees me. Then, spotting my nails, 'I should have known better. Look at the *state* of you, girl.'

'She's been in and out of that bathroom all afternoon,' Nana says, not even looking.

Mum grabs me by the arm and pulls me out of the room. 'Come here,' she says, dragging me towards the bathroom. 'Look at yourself,' she says. '*Look*.'

In the mirror, I am the same as I was before. 'I look supercool,' I say.

'You look like *jailbait*,' she spits.

I ignore her and pat my hair back into place.

'Carmen, sweetheart, you don't understand.' She sits down on the edge of the bath to tell me that Lisa is trying to get back at her, that she's using me. 'What did she tell you about me? Huh? It's all *lies*, Carmen. She lives in a fantasy world. Always has done. She's trying to make you look stupid to get at me. Can't you see that?'

She pauses for breath. 'And I bet she didn't tell you,' she pauses spitefully, 'that you look fat in that top.'

She ignores me until we get back to the flat. 'You know why I left your father? I was *bored*. Bored, bored, bored, *bored*.' She looks at me sideways. 'I thought we could spend the night at home together. Just you and me. Get a takeaway and a video.'

'But, Mum, you *said* I could go.'

'I'll come with you, then.' She stands in front of me, her arms folded. 'Reckon I could still cut it? Will there be any older people there?'

'But, Mum, you *said*,' I repeat, pleading.

'But it's hard for me, meeting new people at my age. You have much more chance than me.' She sighs. 'I thought we were going to be like sisters.'

'You wouldn't enjoy it.'

'Why not? It's not a jelly and ice-cream party, is it? Not dressed like that.'

I shrug. 'It's a girls' party.'

'Oh, and I'm not a girl any more then?'

I don't answer.

# 14

Paisley's house is old. Semi-detached, Victorian, wide stone steps and a glass porch. When Mum pulls up outside she's impressed.

'Well look at that,' she says, sounding surprised. 'Looks like you're making friends in high places. I knew that school was the right place for you. What do her parents do?'

I shrug. 'Dunno,' I say.

'Well find out.'

She's going to come back at half-eleven. 'If you insist on dressing like that then you're not giving me any option,' she says, and waits in the car, the engine idling, until Paisley has opened the door.

'Wow, Carmen. You look *cool.*' Paisley is stoned; her eyes are narrowed to slits. 'We're getting ready.'

Maxine is in the lounge drinking a bottle of Pink Grapefruit 20/20; there's half a joint smouldering in the ashtray. Paisley says her parents are cool with her smoking. 'They're hippies,' she says. 'They do it all the time.'

Her house is a proper home. Squashy sofas, rugs on the walls and bare floorboards.

'Where d'you get your nails done? They're, like, *totally* cool.'

Paisley touches my hair, my tattoos. I tell her about Lisa's stall. 'Ooh, will you take me there? *Please.*'

Maxine looks at me, takes another swig of her drink. 'I want to get changed now, I look *crap* compared to Carmen,' she whines.

'No you don't,' Paisley says.

'Don't be silly,' I say. But I know that when she twists her mouth like that, all mean and jealous, Maxine looks a mess.

'Come upstairs and help me do my make-up.' Paisley grabs my hand and leads me up the big, sweeping staircase to her bedroom.

She shuts the door and moans about Maxine, tells me in whispers how she's too clingy, how they never have fun any more. 'I'd rather be *your* friend.'

Paisley's room is cluttered with girly things. On her dressing table there's a row of Barbie dolls. Roller-Skating Barbie, with tiny roller skates and shiny tights; Horse-Riding Barbie in jodhpurs and tweed jacket; Ballet Barbie in a pink tutu and silk pumps, and a Girl-About-Town Barbie complete with mobile phone and glittery handbag.

Paisley giggles when she sees me looking at them. 'I collect them,' she says.

I pick up Roller-Skating Barbie and bend her legs behind her ears.

'Yoga Barbie,' I say, showing her.

She squeals. 'Oh you're so *funny*, Carmen.'

While Paisley puts on some mascara, I undress Girl-About-Town-Barbie. Her pink plastic body looks perfect: big tits, thin hips. I wish I looked like that. I pick out a

115

pearly bead necklace from the jumble of Paisley's accessories and tie it around her long Barbie neck.

'Suicide Barbie,' I say, holding her up so she swings
like a hanged man.

Paisley looks scared. 'Carmen, that's *disturbing*.'

The boys arrive, bringing a gang with them. Trev, Rich,
Dunc, Matt and Pete. I lose track of which one's which.
Paisley puts Craig David on the stereo, turns down the
lights. She sits on the sofa, holding Carter's hand. Maxine
is in the corner, checking out Dean's tonsils. The gang
hangs around, cracking cans, casting furtive glances,
sitting with their legs splayed like they've got something
uncomfortable between them.

'I brought a few mates,' Carter says. 'Hope you don't
mind. There's more coming later, after the pub.'

I perch on the sofa next to Paisley, feeling conspicuous.
'Who's yer mate?'

'Carmen,' Paisley says, 'the new girl.'

'Oh, aye, didn't recognize you there.' He sticks his hand
out and stares at my chest. 'Gorgeous.' He grabs my
hand tight, squeezing my knuckles.

A few more girls from school turn up. Carter puts a
seventies compilation CD on to try and get people
dancing but no one's drunk enough yet. He offers us
some pills. 'Come on,' he says, 'this party's getting me
down, man.'

Paisley takes one, but I refuse. He shrugs. 'Your loss,'
he says putting one on his tongue and swallowing it with
a swig of beer.

Carter is the kind of boy who likes his girls meaty. He
tells me this as he slides his hand across my breasts. I'm

waiting in the corridor outside Paisley's posh bathroom and I have to clench to stop myself from peeing. Suddenly the house is packed. Loads of people that no one knows have come down the road from the pub. Word of mouth spreads like wildfire on a Saturday night.

'Geddoff,' I say, my arm flailing against the air.

'Come on, honey.' He puckers his lips and presses them against my cheek. 'Get loved up.'

There's a flush and the sound of a door unlocking. I try to squirm away from him, but I'm drunk, woozy and I lurch forwards into him.

His hand slides up my jeans. It tingles where he touches me. He tries to push his hand between my legs.

'You're gorgeous,' he says. 'Anyone ever tell you that before?'

He scratches my cheek with his chin; I can see where glitter has stuck to his stubble.

One of the blokes, Dunc, or Matt, staggers out of the toilet. Carter reaches out a hand to steady him, stop him going headfirst down the stairs. I seize my chance and run into the bathroom, locking the door behind me.

Someone's been sick in the bath and the shower curtain's pulled down, ripped off its hooks. Paisley's parents will go mad. I saw someone stubbing a fag out on the carpet earlier. I lean forwards trying to pee, I want to but I can't. I've drunk too much 20/20, I can taste the sticky pink grapefruit round my lips.

'Come on, bab, 'urry up. I'm busting out here.' It's Carter. 'Come on, I'll be pissing in a plant pot in a minute.'

One of my knots of hair is coming undone. I fix it in the bathroom mirror, shoving the grip in really tight.

When I open the door he surprises me, pushes me

backwards with his hand over my mouth. He rubs his other hand roughly across my breasts.

'Come on, sweetheart,' he says, fumbling with the zip of my jeans.

Then a rush of arms and screams. Someone slaps me. I look up to see Maxine, her face twisted into a sneer. 'You *bitch*,' she says, standing in front of me, breathing hard through her nose. She swipes at my hair, yanking out a hairgrip. 'You *bitch*.' Her eyes are huge and her cheeks are glowing. I think she's done an E. 'I'm gonna tell *Pais*ley.'

Carter is leaning against the wall, hands in the air as if someone is pointing a gun at him.

'Weren't me,' he says. 'She was all over me.'

I sit on the wall outside waiting for Mum. It's freezing. I've left my denim in there somewhere but I'm not going back in to get it.

'This where the party is?'

Two dreadlocked men, tattooed and pierced, are looking at me.

'Yeah.'

They shuffle down the path, one of them calls his friend on his mobile. 'It's just down the road, mate, yeah . . . big house on the right. Music's shit though. Yeh, yeh, we brought some tapes.'

Someone opens the door and music thumps out into the street.

*Take me awaaaay, to your fantasyyyyy*

More groups of people are arriving, walking down the hill from the pub. The music stops abruptly and is replaced by heavy metal rock. Then shouting, the sound of glass breaking and thrash guitars screeching. It goes on for a bit, then suddenly it stops. There's a pause, but only for a second, as if everyone is catching a breath, finding their second wind, then the thumping goes on, only now it's louder. The *duff duff duff duff* of bass turned up too loud.

People spill out on to the front steps. Boys pissing in the bushes behind me. A police car crawls past. I spark a cigarette. I wish Mum would hurry up.

Paisley laughed when Maxine told her about Carter, she looked at me with her eyes huge and far away. It was Maxine who banned me; she pushed me out of the door and told me to piss off. I didn't want to stay anyway. Bunch of losers.

'Carmen! Get in the car. NOW!' When I get in she makes me look in the mirror. My hair is undone and falling around my shoulders in untidy straggles and lipstick is smeared across my face, my chest.

'No point in asking what happened to you, is there?' she says, triumphantly. I sit in the front seat and listen to her going on. 'I thought her parents were going to be here.'

'So did I,' I lie.

When we get round the corner, she pulls up on to the kerb and calls the police.

'That'll sort them,' she says, snapping her phone shut. 'And honestly if I'd known it was going to turn into one of *those* parties I'd never have let you go.'

# 15

I lie on my bed, listening to the wind rushing around the tower. It hisses angrily through the gaps in the windows, making the curtains flap and twitch. I can still feel the mark of Carter's hands across my chest, down my legs. I squeeze my thigh with my fingers until it pinches. I wish I wasn't so fat. If I was thin and beautiful, Carter wouldn't have dared to touch me.

I flick through a copy of *More!* that Mum bought for me, although I've read it a thousand times already. The problem page is full of girls whose boyfriends have left them for their best mates. I'll tell Paisley on Monday that I don't want Carter, that it was all a big mistake. She'll have to believe me. All the answers say that mates are more important than boys.

At the bottom of the page is one short letter that says:

*I've always had a problem with my weight. A few months ago I started to make myself sick after meals and I've got really thin, but now I can't stop and I throw up even when I don't want to. Please help.*

The answer tells her to talk to someone, to phone a helpline, to write to a support group.

I read the letter over and over. I don't know what she's moaning about. At least she got thin.

Dad has phoned to say that I can stop with him over half-term. I won't come back, I'll stay there for ever. Once he's got used to me in the house it'll be fine. I'm sure of it. He says we can play *Gran Turismo* and *Tekken*.

Mentally, I pack my bags, even though there's still a week to go. I'll get Lisa to do my nails specially so I can show him.

Mum says she's pleased. 'It'll be a blessed relief to get some time to myself.'

'Slag!' Maxine says it like she's spitting.

I turn the corner down the corridor towards the cloak-rooms. But Maxine's in front of me already, Paisley behind me, like they did to Kelly. They're both in loads of trouble. Paisley's house got trashed and Maxine's mum found out that she'd done an E. And they're both on report until the end of term for smoking in the toilets.

'Bitch.'

Pain in my side, something poking me in the back. Maxine's got a compass in her hand. My fists clench.

I look at Paisley, pleadingly. 'I don't want him,' I say. 'I never did.'

'Liar!' Maxine sneers. 'I *saw* you trying to cop off with him.'

Paisley won't meet my eye. 'Belly,' she says, 'cry baby.'

'Yeah, fat cow.'

'Carter reckons you're a slapper.'

'You never had a chance with him anyway.'

'Don't know why you bothered.'

'*Slag*,' they say together.

Another punch and this time the point of the compass grazes my skin, a long, thin scratch, that will leave a jagged scar along the back of my hand.

121

She says that I shouldn't dress like a firework until I know how to control the explosion. 'You're only fourteen,' she says. 'You just have to learn to be more *poised*. And you're banned from seeing Lisa. D'you hear me? *Banned.*'

She's bought me a dress. Red Indian style, with feather and bead tassels and embroidered trim. Same as the one in the catalogue, except close up the material is scratchy, see-through, flimsy, like the crêpe paper we had at primary school for making Christmas decorations.

'It's horrible.'

'C'mon, try it on.'

I pull off my top reluctantly while she unpacks her bags and spreads the dress out on the bed. I'm shivering, though I'm not especially cold. I wrap my arms around myself, try to stand behind her, waiting for her to turn round and look.

'Pfffft.' She blows out through her teeth. I pull my stomach in. 'You're not getting any thinner are you?' She rummages in her bags. 'If you try this on underneath, it will hold you in, give you a nice shape.' She holds up a box. Support Girdle it says on the front.

It's made of hard, shiny elastic. 'It's like having an extra muscle,' she says. 'And so discreet. Come on, I'll help you put it on.'

I step into it as she holds it open, sprung apart like a trap.

'Don't struggle,' she says, as it starts to stick at the top of my thighs. 'There.' She lets it snap into place over my stomach.

'Owwww.'

I wriggle uncomfortably in my new skin. It makes my stomach like a trampoline.

'You could bounce rocks off that now,' my mother says, as if reading my thoughts.

To go with the dress, she's bought me a pair of moccasin-style shoes. Brown suede with blunted ends and no heels. They look kind of trendy, but not on me. When I look in the mirror my legs, already cut short by the skirt of the dress, seem to end in flat, clumsy stumps, the flesh in between pasty tree trunks. I put my baseball cap on again, just to ruin the effect even more.

'Put your legs together, that's better. You're not wearing trousers, you know, and come on, take your cap off. I want to brush your hair.' And we'll have to do something about those nails. They don't match at all.'

My hair is too long. I want it cut shorter but Mum says I'll regret it. She pulls a nylon brush down hard through the tangles.

'Owww. Mu-*um*, it hurts.'

But she's on a mission. Glitter falls out like dandruff across my shoulders.

'I don't care if it hurts. You're *my* daughter, and I'll have you looking nice. Not like some fifty-pence slapper, like that sister of mine.'

'What happened to your hand?' Lisa touches the scratch with the end of a paintbrush.

'Fell over,' I say.

'How was your party? Did you knock 'em dead?'

I shrug and tell her that I'm going to visit Dad for half-term. 'He's coming to get me tomorrow.'

She raises her eyebrows. 'Brian's coming all the way down here?'

I nod. 'I wanted you to do my nails to show him.'

'Ah. I see.'

She takes off the beige polish that Mum put on. 'What kind of thing d'you think he'd like?' she asks. 'I don't know him very well, you know. Your mother would never introduce us to him properly. I think she thought we were too scummy.'

'You're not scummy,' I say, indignant. I don't know why Mum's so cross with Lisa, she's nice.

She smiles. 'Don't you worry, she's just having a funny turn. We'll all still be here when she comes back round again.'

She does my nails a glittery camouflage, with swirls of olive green and silver.

'There you go,' she says. 'Little soldier.'

# 16

The first day of half-term and it's raining. *Pissing it*, Grandad said, before he went to the pub. I'm at Nana's with my homework, watching telly in the gloom. Dad cancelled yesterday afternoon. An urgent order had come in, he said. 'I'm going to be working all week. I won't be able to spend any time with you, I'm sorry.'

'You see,' Mum said, 'it's that Moira. Do anything for her he would.'

When I spoke to him on the phone Mum stood behind me, rubbing her hands, chin nearly on my shoulder.

'What's he saying? What's he saying?' she whispered so loudly I could hardly hear his voice.

'How's my favourite teenager?' he said.

'Fine,' I said, my voice a squeak, trying not to cry.

'Really?' He didn't sound convinced. 'I'll be down your way in a couple of weeks. I'll bring you something nice. I'm sorry. OK, sugarpuff? You keep smiling. OK?'

Mum snatched the receiver back off me.

'I won't have you giving her false hopes, Brian,' she said. 'You *promised* to have her at half-term. And now my mother's got to look after her. At her age.'

He said something I couldn't hear and my mother laughed too loudly, sarcastically. 'Trouble with you Brian, is you're a bloody *liar*.'

Grandad's hedge has become a public nuisance. A man from the council has been round, told him to cut it down.

'I pay my taxes, same as everybody else,' he said. 'I have rights, you know. *Rights.*'

Nana's given up nagging him because it doesn't do any good. 'He'll cut it down soon enough,' she says. 'He'll have to.'

It's *Dynasty* week on UK Gold. The whole series from start to finish in one week. 'Love this programme,' she says, cracking a humbug between her teeth. 'I thought we could go to the shops in a bit, get some treats.'

She shifts in her seat, her thighs rippling under the thin material of her dress. She pushes her glasses up her nose and leans closer to the TV, reaching over for the bag of sweets and sitting them on her lap like a cat.

Down the road from Nana's house there's a row of shops. A newsagent, a curry house, an off-licence and a mini supermarket. Nana has taken her wheely trolley and her walking stick. She wheezes when she walks and the day-light has made the lenses of her glasses go a smoky brown.

'Oooh, I don't get out enough,' she says, stopping at the crossing to catch her breath.

The supermarket is small and overflowing with stuff. Boxes of apples, oranges, peppers, mushrooms, onions, potatoes are banked up outside. Nana walks right past as if she doesn't even notice them. Inside it smells weird. I wrinkle my nose.

'Curry powder,' Nana says, looking at me. 'That's what you can smell.'

There's stuff piled right up to the ceiling. The aisles are only just wide enough for Nana to squeeze down them.

'Where are the chocolate biscuits?' she asks me.

'In front of you, look,' I say.

She peers over the bulk of her belly. 'Ooh, yes, get two packets of those bourbons, there's a love. I don't think I can quite reach them.'

In fact, if she bent over to reach them, she would probably knock over the shelf of toilet rolls, nappies and Tampax behind her.

'How about some of those for our tea? While Grandad's not looking?' She points to a pyramid of Pot Noodles.

I shrug. 'Whatever.'

'Curry or chicken?'

'Don't mind.'

She puts two of each in her basket. 'Save you making the wrong decision now.'

Everything is neon colours and plastic packets. At the chiller cabinet she picks up a few packets of processed cheese slices and a tray of ready cooked sausages. Next to the cheap cartons of orange juice is a whole shelf of fluorescent bottles of Sunny Delight.

'What flavour d'you want?' she asks.

I shrug and she puts two bottles of strawberry in her basket.

There are no other customers in the shop but I'm embarrassed anyway. Under the striplights Nana's skin looks blotchy and saggy. Her fingers are fat bananas, like something a kid might draw. She touches everything, looking at the descriptions on all the packets: *high in calcium*, *great for kids!*, *snack size*, *ready in minutes!*, *quick and convenient*. When her hands get to the pasties and the cooked meat I have to look away.

The man at the till raises his eyebrows.

'Put that little lot on my slate will you, Mr Mahmood? I'll pay you come pension day.'

Mr Mahmood narrows his eyes. 'You owe me twenty pounds already.'

'It's my granddaughter,' she says, looking at me. 'Half-term.'

For a moment I think Mr Mahmood might say no. 'So long as you pay next week. This is a shop, not a bank.'

'Oh, come on. I always pay, don't I?'

Mr Mahmood looks away and starts jabbing the prices into his till, giving the things he's counted to Nana to pack into her trolley bag.

'That's thirteen forty-two,' he says after the last packet of Maltesers has been accounted for. 'That's thirty-three forty-two altogether.' He looks at Nana for a moment as if he expects her to hand over the money. Then he gets out a notebook and writes in it. 'Sign here,' he says, tapping the page with a pen.

'Monday,' Nana says, her eyelashes fluttering behind her glasses. '*Promise.*'

When we get back she puts everything out on the coffee table in bowls.

'Help yourself, love,' she says, picking up the remote control and flicking through the channels before settling back on UK Gold again.

I eat a Smartie really slowly, letting the chocolate melt on my tongue. Nana gets stuck into a tube of Pringles. She's absorbed in her programme, face wobbling as she munches. Watching her makes me feel sick. *I'm like that*, I think. *That's how I look.*

'I'm bored.'

'Don't you have any homework to do, love?' She says, taking a swig of strawberry Sunny Delight.

*I must try harder*, I write, pressing the biro into my biology book, *not to eat*. It is this which is at the root of my problems, I have decided. Not Mum and Dad, or Nana or Kelly or Maxine and Paisley, but this: my puffy face, my swelling breasts, my belly. If I was beautiful I could have everything I wanted. I could stay with Dad and Mum wouldn't hate me.

I poke myself with my finger, digging the nail into the skin until it leaves a crescent shape in my flesh. *I hate you*, I say to myself under my breath. *I hate you*.

I rip the page out, but the shape of the words has pushed through the soft paper. I trace my fingertips along the indents. The m of *must* has ripped the paper of the sheet beneath.

When I get the bus back into town, it's already dark. Rain splatters the bus windows as it squeaks and creaks its way down the hill. I feel sickly but not sick. A kind of acid taste in my mouth. Lights on the cranes underneath the Rotunda wink against the black sky. They look like a monster, a spider, chewing up the town in slow motion. If I close my eyes I can almost hear the crunch of its jaws, rubble falling from the sides of its mouth in long drools of concrete and dust.

# 17

'We're moving,' Mum says. 'I found our new house today.'

She's got paint catalogues out, looking at colours. 'What kind of colour d'you want in your bedroom? I thought maybe a pink or a green.'

'Where is it?' I ask.

'Not far,' she says. 'It's new. And they do the decorating before you move in. We'll go and see it soon if you want. For keeps this time, promise.'

'But I like it here,' I say.

'You've changed your tune,' she says, not looking up. Then under her breath, '*Teenagers.*'

As well as a new house, Mum has a new friend. A woman from work called Victoria. Victoria is thin as a stick and beautiful. She comes up from London a few times a month to check on the shop. She has glossy blonde hair, pink, French-polished nails and something my mum calls class.

We are meeting Victoria in the Circle bar that has opened across the road from our tower block. Mum won't invite her into the flat, she says it's too shabby. She's made me put on my new dress and before we came out she spent half an hour plaiting my hair into two fat pigtails.

'Maria, how *lovely* to see you again,' Victoria says, arranging herself on the hard metal seat. 'And this is Carmen,' she says, blowing cigarette smoke in my face. 'Such a *lovely* name. Simply my *favourite* opera.'

Apart from her boots, which are black, Victoria is all gold. Gold leather jacket, gold jewellery, skinny beige trousers and a tight golden top that shows off her belly button which is pierced with a little gold stud. She looks like someone has bent pipe cleaners to make her sit down. I am probably twice her size and she is probably more than twice my age.

'You look quite *fabulous*,' she says.

'Thank you,' I say.

'Oh,' she says, 'I meant your mother.' She pauses to take another suck on her cigarette. 'But you look *great*. That Native American look is so *in* at the moment. I'm so glad I persuaded the stores to buy them. You couldn't move for feathers and moccasins in Milan last year and now we can't get them made up quick enough. We had to get on the phone to the factory, tell them to hire more workers. Isn't that *wonderful*?' She clasps her hands together. 'Now we employ whole *towns* in Papua New Guinea. All that *money* we're making for their communities. It's marvellous, *marvellous*.'

Mum smiles approvingly.

'So you're *moving*, Maria? Tell me *all* about it.' Watching her, I realize that Victoria is the kind of woman who breathes rather than talks.

The waiter comes over. He's young and spotty with a white apron tied at an angle across his waist. 'Would you like to see the menus?'

'Yes, please,' Mum says.

'Not for me,' says Victoria at exactly the same time.

131

'I've been eating like a *pig* all day.' She smiles, baring her teeth. 'I'll have a mineral water. But don't let me stop *you.*'

Mum has gone a bit red. 'No, it's fine,' she says, 'I'll just have a mineral water, with a touch of lime,' and before I can protest, she adds, 'for both of us.'

'So *tell* me, Maria,' Victoria says, leaning across the table conspiratorially, her gold shoulder rudely in my face. 'Are you coming down for London Fashion Week this year?'

'She's so lovely,' Mum says, as we navigate the puddles in the underpass. 'She goes to parties with Kate Moss and Meg Matthews.'

'Mmmm,' I say, wondering if we're going to get any supper, glad because once we're home I can take my dress off. Mum seems not to have noticed that Victoria spent the whole night asking her questions without waiting to hear the answer.

'If I was young and single, I'd be like her,' she says.

The landing light on our floor needs fixing. The neon flickers faster than you can blink, making everything seem out of focus. There's a strong smell of fresh cigarettes and I can see a figure, slumped on the floor of the corridor outside the flat.

'Orright, Maria?' It's Billy.

'Who let you in? What you doing sitting outside?' Mum asks, the questions running into each other, she says them so fast.

'Still got the key in't I? It is still my flat. Anyway, you changed the locks or I'd be sat inside, wouldn't I? What d'ya do that for? No need to get new locks put in.'

132

'Didn't know who else'd been here did I? Wouldn't trust some of the scum you hang out with further 'n I could spit on them.' Mum's voice has dropped a few notes; she sounds flatter, broader than she did with Victoria.

'Oh, come on, Maria, don't be such a snob.'

'I'm not. I've got Carmen to think about,' she says, using my name with a flourish.

'Actually, it was *Carmen* I came to see. Not you.' Upright, Billy fills the whole corridor. He's wearing a blue suit in shiny, sparkly material with a dark velvet trim on the jacket, and a pair of shoes with thick crepe soles.

'And what's with the Elvis routine?' Mum demands.

'Hollywood night at the restaurant,' he says. 'Everyone dressed up as their favourite *staaaar...*' He sways towards us as he says this, and I notice a can of Stella by the wall where he's been sitting.

'Are you drunk, Billy?'

'Might be,' he says, smiling. 'You gonna make us a cuppa tea then or what?'

Mum sends me to bed while Billy goes for a pee. 'He's drunk, sweetheart, you don't want to listen to him going on. Go and do your homework.'

I lie in bed listening to them talking in the lounge. I can't hear what they're saying, Mum has put some music on: *Ibiza Party Anthems* that she bought last week. She said she's going to go next year with the girls from work, that I can stay with Nana for a week. 'Cheryl and Denise have both got kids and they go every year,' she said, as if I were accusing her of something.

I'm starving, my belly feels like it's caving in. I run my hand across it to see if it's got any flatter. I haven't even got any emergency chocolate: I ate it all last night.

I flick through the copy of *Elle* that has been on my floor for weeks. It's full of women like Victoria: gold women, thin women, women who feel hungry all the time.

I check myself in the mirror to see if I look any thinner. I suck my cheeks in, giving myself cheekbones like Kate Moss. Good, I think, that's better.

In my diary I write:

*Slice of toast, orange juice, tea, mineral water, NO lunch, NO supper.*

I underline the NO in red pen so Mum will see.

# 18

I stand on the scales in the bathroom. The window faces out on to the corridor, hidden by frosted glass and a dirty green curtain. It's the only part of the flat where you can't hear the traffic, the howl of wind round the building.

I look down, gritting my teeth. Eight stone two. It's more than last week.

'I'm *fat*,' I hear myself saying, miserably, hopelessly. I look in the mirror. My face has gone hot and red, I feel like I'm going to explode. 'I'm *fat*.' It sizzles under my skin, thick yellow layers of it, puffing me up, pushing me out, making me massive.

'Metabolism,' she says. 'Metabolism. Does anyone know what that means?'

Paisley and Maxine are giggling. 'Is that like when you're really fat, Miss?'

Miss Burton arches an eyebrow. 'I'm not sure what you mean.'

'Like Kelly, Miss.' More giggles. Next to me Kelly tenses.

'Paisley Harries and Maxine Miles, you will see me after class. Now. *Metabolism*. What is it?'

I doodle on my notebook. I can't concentrate. I haven't

eaten anything all day. I draw stick men and women. THIN I write underneath in big black letters. THIN.

My stomach feels like it's caving in. My head hurts. And as I get off the bus it's like I've got nothing to do with it: one moment I'm about to turn the corner to the flat, the next I've ordered pie and chips and a chocolate milk from the chippie on the Bristol Road.

I eat really fast, like I can trick myself into forgetting that I wasn't going to eat anything today.

I drink the chocolate milk anyway. I don't see that it's going to make any difference.

I look at myself in the window; my freckled cheeks are puffy like balloons. I am stupid, pathetic, dumb, like Kelly.

I want to be sick.

When I get back to the flat Mum's in the bathroom.

'I'm having a bath,' she says when I knock on the door. 'You're not desperate, are you?'

Yes, I think, *yes*.

'No,' I say.

I watch cartoons. I can feel my stomach growing, rising into a bloated, doughy mound. I tell myself that this is the last time. That I will eat nothing tomorrow. I think of the girl on the problem page. *I started to make myself sick after meals and I've got really thin.*

Mum comes into the living room with a towel wrapped around her body. The bones in her shoulders look like coat hangers.

'I'm going out with Victoria tonight. You'll be all right on your own, won't you?'

She looks at me, her head on one side.

'Yeah.' I stare at the TV.

The bathroom smells of her. Of perfume and antiseptics. The room is humid; the mirror steamed up so my reflection is just a haze. I run the taps so she won't hear.

My mouth fills with saliva as I push my fingers into my mouth. I retch, but nothing comes up and my eyes start to water.

When I try again the milkshake comes up first. Then clumps of pie and chips. It scalds my throat, my tongue, makes my eyes water, my nose hurt.

When there's nothing left, I flush, stand up, holding on to the sink, drink water from the toothmug smeary with toothpaste. My belly feels better now. Flatter. Though I should have done it sooner, before so many calories soaked in.

When I sit down to pee, there's blood in my knickers; I have to use toilet roll to stop it because Mum hasn't got any Tampax. 'I haven't bought any of those things for ages,' she says, waving her hand vaguely, giving me some money.

She inspects herself in the mirror before she goes out, smoothing down her hair, wiping an imaginary smudge from her cheek. There is a fuzz of soft, downy hair on her face. She touches her neck self-consciously.

'Like a chicken,' she says. She turns ninety degrees and studies herself sideways, her hipbones jut where her bum should be. 'Look at me,' she says. 'Look. I'm an old *hag*.'

Later in bed, I hear her coming in. There's someone with her: a deeper voice, a man's voice. I wonder if it's Billy. I sit up in bed, pull my knees to my chest. Someone trips over the coffee table and there's a crash and a giggle and Mum saying *shhhhhhh*.

I know they're doing it. Mum makes noises like a kitten mewling. The bed creaks, a man grunts. I light a cigarette and smoke it in the dark, flicking ash in an empty Coke can, watching the tip glow red in front of my nose.

When I go to the bathroom to clean my teeth I meet him in the corridor, a towel round his waist. He has gold rings on all his fingers and a thick gold chain round his wrist. I push past him as if he isn't there, keep my eyes on the carpet, fold my arms across my chest. He sniffs and lumbers back to Mum's room. As I lock the door I can hear the springs of her bed creaking as he gets back into it.

In the morning I wait until I hear him leave before I get out of bed. Mum is running a bath. She looks tired, her eyes have bruised, purple lines underneath them.

'Don't you start,' she says, seeing me mooching in the corridor. 'When you've had a husband you get used to having a man about the place. You'll learn.'

# 19

Billy's invited us over for supper. When I ask why we're going Mum says she wants to keep him sweet because our new house won't be ready for another month. 'I don't want him turfing us out before it's ready,' she tells me. 'And don't eat too much. Just have a starter instead of a main course and NO pudding. OK?'

We walk across town to get the bus up the Hagley Road towards Ladywood. Mum's wearing her new leather trousers and a gold jacket like Victoria's. She's been to the Suncentre this week too, her skin looks orangey and her eyebrows have been plucked and pencilled into sharp razored peaks.

When we get to Steers, Billy's waiting outside.

'I thought we could go somewhere uptown,' he says.

'I thought we were eating here.'

'I wouldn't have you eat in here, Maria, what d'you take me for? Some kind of cheapskate? Only the best for you, now you are moving up' – he raises his eyes to the sky – 'in the world. Your carriage awaits.' He points with a sweep of his arm to a silvery car parked on the gravel nearby. 'Even got a driver for tonight, we have.'

A heavyset mound of a man waves out of the window. 'Orright, Maria?'

Mum looks taken aback. '*Dickie*. Didn't know you were

still on the scene.' Then to Billy, 'I wish you'd *said*, we could have met you in town.'

'And saved me the chance to spoil you a bit? Welcome you back? Don't you like being treated nice?'

Mum blushes and looks confused. She pecks him on the cheek. 'A silver Jag, eh?'

We sit in the back of the car, the three of us, Mum in the middle. Dickie's got a uniform on, proper peaked cap and everything.

'What's with all this then?' Mum says, pointing through the glass at the driver. 'Rich enough to employ *servants* now, are we?'

We go to a restaurant in Brindley Place. All the fittings shine in a classy kind of way: marble, glass and chrome. There are dried flowers and twigs in vases on the tables and big, abstract paintings on the wall – expanses of muted blues and greens.

It's full of people talking quietly. A few stop to look at us as we walk in.

'If I'd known we were coming here I'd've worn a different outfit,' Mum hisses in my ear. 'Hundred pound a head they charge. Choose something really expensive.'

The waiter sits us at a table in the corner, Mum insisting that she has the seat that faces the room. 'I can't bear not being able to look at people. That's the point of eating out, isn't it?' She smooths her hair self-consciously and looks Billy in the eye. 'So how come you're able to afford all this finery then, Billy? Been robbing banks?'

Billy laughs. 'No, I've been meking money.' He taps a cigarette out of its packet. 'Food, Maria. *Food*. It's a wonderful thing.' He tells us that he's been making more money than he knows what to do with. That he's booked up till Easter. 'People think they're getting a good deal. *'All U Can Eat? Only ten quid? That can't be right!'* They think they're getting something for nothing, like. None of the poncey portions you get in here. Proper stuffing and as much of it as you like! 'S brilliant.' Despite the cool, almost chilly temperature of the restaurant Billy is sweating. 'It's amazing,' he says. 'Amazing. I've never been so loaded in my life.'

A waitress comes with menus, wine lists. Billy orders bottles in exaggerated French, curling the 'r' of 'Corbières' around his tongue. Mum is watching him, her mouth slightly open, she has a cigarette in her hand that she has forgotten to light.

'Well, isn't that *great*?' she says eventually, not sounding very convinced.

'I know, but that's not the best bit.' He lowers his voice. 'You see, no one ever eats ten quid's worth of food. Even your fattest, grossest, most' – he puffs his cheeks out – '*fat* bastard can't eat more than two quid's worth. Most people eat less than a quid's worth and they can't move. And it's costing me pennies, Maria, pennies. And it's all shit. All of it. Forget the four food groups. All cheap. All fried. All protein or carbohydrate. And because it's salty and there's no discounts on the drinks, I make a fortune on the bar. Food. Who'd've thought it, eh? Better money than dealing. And it's legal.' He looks at the menu. 'What you going to have? The fish in here is very good.'

I try to read the menu but it's all in French. 'What's a confit, Mum?'

'Ahhh. The *confee*,' Billy says, putting on his stupid French accent and staring at Mum. He's grinning like Joker from the Batman film. 'And what about you, Maria?

I think the fish for you perhaps, something low in the fat stakes would suit you.'

Mum looks at him really hard. 'Billy? Are you *on* something?'

He looks round the restaurant for the waiter, snaps his fingers. 'Over here!'

Mum groans. 'For God's sake. Why does everything have to be a Jack Nicholson routine with you? People are *looking*.'

'Garçon,' Billy continues. The waiter's amused, he stands with his pad ready. 'For these lovely ladies. We'll have one fish, one chicken and I'll have the steak, medium rare.'

'Very good, sir.'

When the waiter has gone Billy looks at us. 'He went to school with Dave's brother. Little Pete – remember him?'

'No.' Mum has her arms folded across her chest. I'm half expecting her to walk out.

'Oh, come on, Maria, I thought this was why you came back. For a bit of class, a bit of *sophistication*. All the things you said we never used to have in Birmingham.'

'Don't take the piss, Billy,' she hisses. 'Not in front of the child.'

'Oh, I'm *sorry*, lady lah di dah.'

Billy sniffs, gets a dirty handkerchief out of his pocket and blows his nose loudly.

'I don't see why you always have to be so bloody *obnoxious*.'

He inspects the contents of his handkerchief then screws it in a ball and stuffs it back in his pocket. 'I thought that was the point. Never mind the bollocks and all that. Being obnoxious, it's *rock and roll*, Maria.'

142

'For you and Lisa maybe. Not me, Billy, *never* me. I'm not one of *your* gang.'

'Still haven't seen her yet, have you?'

Mum stiffens. 'Why? She been bitching about me?'

'Has it occurred to you she might want to see you?'

'She knows where to find me.' Mum squeezes her lips together, exaggerating the lines around her mouth. She looks old and mean.

'If you don't watch it, the wind will change and you'll get stuck like that, Maria.'

Mum harrumphs and opens her mouth. She stops when she sees the waiter weaving through the tables, plates balanced along his arm like an acrobat. Our food is arranged and garnished like pictures from a cookery book. Mum's fish has still got its head; a steely eye looks up from her plate. She pokes it with her knife.

'I can't deal with this,' she says.

# 20

She's thrown my baseball cap away and it's cold and drizzly outside. I finger the tenner that Billy gave me, folded up to the size of a stamp in my pocket. My stomach is sore. I had to throw up twice after dinner last night because Billy insisted that I have a pudding.

Without stopping to think about it, I walk up the hill towards the city centre, past the bus stop to school. The shops aren't open yet and town is full of the shushing of road sweepers clearing leaves out of the gutters.

I buy a pack of ten Silk Cut from a newsagent in the underpass. I look at the display of chocolate. The bright wrappers, the gooey toffee chocolate taste that would coat my mouth like a comfort blanket. I turn away before I'm tempted.

Huddling in the doorway outside the Odeon cinema, I watch the crowds building up into one big stream of people, heels clack-clacking, hurrying their way to work. I press back against the glass. A man with a dog on a scruffy lead squats down in the doorway next me, spreads his coat on the floor in front of him and puts a pile of *Big Issue* magazines on top.

'*Big Isshoo*,' he shouts. His dog sidles up to me, sniffing my ankles. I pretend not to notice.

Mums says only drug addicts and mad people end up

on the street. She never gives them money or buys their magazines. 'It only makes things worse for them in the end,' she tells me. I look at the man out the corner of my eye, clutching my change in my fist in case he tries to rob me. When he turns and smiles showing a row of broken teeth, I look away and push off into the surging crowd, letting the momentum carry me all the way up the street to Victoria Square.

I sit by the fountain for a bit, watching pigeons fighting over scraps of food round the bins. The statue of the woman at the top of the fountain is fat. Reclining with her thick legs crossed at the ankle, her hand resting across her lap. Mum said that it was grotesque, in this day and age. 'Fat just isn't beautiful any more. If all the girls looked like that floozy we'd be out of business in a day.'

'Can't you just make bigger clothes?' I asked, for once failing to follow her logic.

'Of course we could,' she said. 'But we don't want to. Fat people put customers off. I mean, we're not Evans or Etam, for God's sake. Our clothes are classy, and classy women are thin. I'm sorry, Carmen, but there's the truth of it – you'll see.'

I look at the women rushing to work. Lots of tight, shiny trousers, neat leather jackets, business suits. They move sleekly, in one elegant movement as if they all have the same body. I snuggle into my Adidas bench coat that I got Dad to buy me, and light another fag. I like the taste of them now and they stop you from feeling hungry.

When the morning rush is over the drizzle turns to rain. My fag fizzles out; water runs in little trickles under my sweater, down the collar of my school shirt. I plunge my hands deep into my jacket pockets and walk back down New Street. I'll go and find Lisa, get her to make me a cup of tea. I'll pretend it's teacher-training day or something.

I get lost on the way to the markets. They've boarded up the underpasses and signs saying *Danger Demolition* are everywhere. I try to cut across St Martin's Circus but all the entrances are boarded up.

On the signs it says the markets have moved to temporary accommodation somewhere nearby, but I can't work out how to get there from here. The rain is pelting now, thick splashes that make sodden puddles on the greasy pavements. The water is brown with brick dust and mud. My trainers start leaking and my feet squelch stickily inside them.

Air conditioning blasts hot air out into the street. Mum's shop is narrow, with a tall front window that has dresses arranged on wires, like they're floating up towards the second floor. Mum is standing by the counter talking to a girl behind the till who has a face the colour of red cheese.

When she sees me, her expression freezes. 'Carmen? Is that you? What are you doing here? Look at the state of you.' She pulls the hood of my jacket down.

'Felt sick,' I say.

'Show your face, girl. Why are you wearing your trainers? I thought you put your shoes on this morning? Those trainers have got holes in. I should have made you throw them away. What are you doing here?'

'I'm sick,' I say again.

'Oh.' She looks flustered and smiles at cheese-powder features. 'Excuse me a moment, won't you, Theresa?'

146

She grabs me round the waist, pushing me towards the door, out past the rails of winter coats and shiny Christmas dresses. From behind it must look like she's giving me a hug. 'Go *away*. You can't come here,' she hisses.

'But I've been *sick*,' I say. I wish I could faint or something. I try and wobble, go floppy on her. Outside the rain gurgles greedily down the street.

'Look at this weather,' she says. Her arm is tight around my waist. 'I suppose you can wait until it stops.' She looks dubiously at the sky. 'If it ever bloody does. Why didn't you tell me you were feeling ill this morning?'

'It only came on when I was on the bus.'

She touches my forehead. Her hands are freezing. 'Well you haven't got a temperature. Come on, you can sit in my office for a bit.'

She seems to come from nowhere, barrelling round the corner, walking from side to side like a duck, plastic rain cap tied over her greying hair. She's carrying shopping bags from Tesco's, Sainsbury's, Marks and Spencer's, Asda, they're all torn with material poking out of them. The left side of her face is disfigured, purple with a birthmark that runs across the whole of her cheek and down her neck.

'Excuse me,' she says, pushing past us. I catch a breath of pee and stale chips.

Mum makes a noise, a kind of high-pitched croak. When I turn round I can see the woman has made her way across the shop to the changing rooms, a couple of winter coats flung over her arm.

'Excuse me! Excuse me!' Mum is waving uselessly at

her back but she disappears into the changing room before Mum can stop her.

Mum wants Theresa to go in. A couple of women come out of the changing rooms, give their clothes back and walk out the shop.

'We're losing customers,' Mum hisses.

'I think we should call the police,' Theresa says. She gets her tan out of a bottle. I can see where it's gone all streaky at the back of her neck.

'No, no. I'll sort this out. Carmen, darling, make yourself useful. Go and see what she's doing.' Mum and Theresa both look at me. I wiggle my toes in my soggy trainers. Mum flips the hood up on my jacket. 'Go on.'

Through the curtain is a small, cold room, partitioned off into cubicles. There is a full-length mirror at one end and a chair with a couple of copies of *FHM* for boyfriends.

She's standing in front of the mirror, not bothering with the privacy of a cubicle. Her figure is round as a beachball, and she's struggling to move her unwieldy arms out of the sleeves of her pink dress. There's bags all over the floor.

'Orrighht, love,' she says when she sees me. She smiles, her cheeks knotting into apples. 'Couldn't give us a hand could ya? Here,' she hands me a sleeve of the dress, 'if you'd just pull that out in front of me like that.' She twists her wrist out of narrow cuffs. 'Wonderful ta-a. They don't make clothes big enough these days, do they? Not for growing girls like you and me. Trouble with me, when I stopped growing up I started growing out instead.' She laughs and pulls the dress down. 'Here, help us undo the zip,' she says, turning her back to me.

When I'm done she stands up, leaving her dress in a

puddle, and waddles towards the mirror. She's filthy, her hands blackened and her legs streaked with mud. Her skin is saggy and veiny, her breasts hang down nearly to her waist. The birthmark is livid against her white skin. I don't know where to look.

'We-ell, there's a sight for sore eyes,' she says. 'What d'you reckon? Do I look orright?'

I don't know what to say.

'I know, hardly God's gift.' She laughs wheezily.

She picks one of the coats off the rail and wraps it around herself. It won't do up and she mutters something about dolls and disgraceful.

The other coat does just about do up and she twirls it in front of the mirror. It's a long frock coat with a weighted skirt, the kind that sweeps around the legs. 'There's lovely. I'll take it,' she says. 'Won't bother taking it off, they can sort me out at the till.' She gathers up her bags, leaving the pink dress on the floor. 'They can give that to charity.'

'Carmen!' Mum's voice filters through the curtain. 'Carmen! What's going on in there?'

'Look—' I start, realizing that my voice is little more than a whisper.

'Cynthia, call me Cynthia. C'mon then, we better get on with it. She's waiting.' She fumbles in her bag and brings out a fistful of five-pound notes. 'I've got good money.'

At the till Mum tells Cynthia that she'll have to take the coat off so they can remove the security tag. 'I'm sorry.'

Cynthia looks bemused. 'Why? I've got good money.' She throws fivers all over the cash desk, crumpled up like little tissues. 'Can't be bothered going back in there. It's

149

depressing, All those mirrors. I'll take it off here if you like.' She starts to unbutton the coat.

'*NO!*' Mum screeches, then steadies herself. 'No. It's all right.' She tells Theresa to ring in £199 and to check all the notes under the UV light.

Cynthia sets off all the alarms when she leaves the shop and it takes Mum ages to switch them off.

She comes back to the till, shaking her head. 'God, wasn't she horrible? You would have thought she could get plastic surgery these days. And *you* didn't have to stare like that, Carmen. Poor woman.'

# 21

'Good,' she says, looking at the scales. 'That's more like it.' Her fingers are like twigs. The bones of her hands are gnarled and knotted, the skin almost transparent. She is trembling slightly. She looks in the mirror and frowns. 'Look at that chin,' she says, tugging at the skin on her throat. 'Funny, isn't it, how it's the first place to show and the last place to go.'

There are lots of ugly things about my body. I have written them down to remind me what I have to do, of the mountainous task that lies ahead of me.

*Hair – too long, too frizzy.*

*Face – too freckled, too fat.*

*Chin – FAT.*

*Shoulders and arms – FAT.*

*Chest – too big, too FAT. (Clothes hang better on a flat chest.)*

*Belly –*

Here I have to stop to punch it. It sticks out too much, bulges, makes me look pregnant. It should be flat.

*Nails – tatty. (Need to manicure.)*

Mum knocks on the door. 'Hurry up, sweetheart, or we'll be late.'

We're going to Nana's. Mum says she's been com-
plaining that we haven't been to visit and she wants to
make arrangements for Christmas. 'Why, I don't know,
because it's only November. She'll be buying food in
already I expect, stupid woman.'

'Why don't you cut it down then?' Mum says. 'You could
get someone in while he's down the pub.'

Nana shrugs and looks at her orthopaedic shoes. The
hedge is taller than the house now, the tops of the ferns
waving in the breeze, high above the chimneys. It's
Leylandii, grows faster than weeds, even in the winter.

'Have some cake, love,' Nana holds a plate out, wedges
of cake arranged on it. Mum holds her hand up.

'No thanks, Mum,' she says. 'We've just eaten.'

Nana puts the plate down on the table. I look at the
cake while they talk. I am so hungry. I can imagine
the taste of it, the texture, the cream, the sugar, the cocoa.
My body feels hollow. Just a little bit, just a little . . .

'Carmen! What are you doing?'

'I haven't eaten the whole piece,' I say.

Mum gives me a look.

'Have a bit more, love,' Nana says.

Only a thin streak of bile comes up. A swirl of chocolaty
goo. I scrape my knuckles on my teeth, trying to get my
hand out of the way.

I look at my face in the mirror. My eyes are a bit
watery, so I sit on the toilet seat and wait for them to dry.

The doorbell goes. I can hear voices in the corridor.
Mum's voice distant and then just outside the door.

'Carmen. Carmen, hurry up. We've got to go. *Now.*'

I turn the tap on, splash my hands under the water. Flush again in case there's anything left.

When I open the door Mum is standing outside and I can see Lisa in front of Nana peering down the corridor. She's wearing a shiny red mac with a matching check handbag.

'So that's what you look like then, Maria. I've been wondering. Hiya, kiddo,' she says, winking at me.

'Come on, we're going,' Mum says, not turning to look.

'You can't avoid me for ever,' Lisa says. 'We're living in the same city now. In fact,' she says, 'believe it or not, we're standing in the same house.'

'Not in front of the child,' Mum says. She's trembling.

'I'm not a child,' I say.

'Don't be difficult, Carmen.' Mum shoots me an evil look.

'Come on, Maria, can't we kiss and make up?'

Lisa folds her arms across her chest. Mum's eyes are scary, wild.

'The wind will change and your face will get stuck like that, Maria.'

'I'm not talking to you if you're only going to be insulting.'

Lisa bites her lip. 'What *happened* to you?'

'I grew up,' Mum says, viciously. 'I got real.'

'At least come to my party.' She gives us both invitations, posh cream card with glitter around the edge. 'I'm opening the new salon. Billy's coming, Annmarie. All the old crowd.'

I take one, but Mum knocks her hand away and tugs me towards the front door. As I pass Nana she presses the cakes into my hand. 'Take them with you, for later, love,' she whispers.

'Temper, temper,' Lisa calls after us, all sarky. The air crackles.

'Girls,' Nana says. 'Please, there's no need.'

'Oh shut up, shut up, you stupid, *stupid* woman. What do you know about anything?' Mum snarls. 'Come on, Carmen.' She pulls me out of the house, hurting my wrist.

When we get to the car she grabs the bag.

'Give,' she says, '*Give.*'

She slides into the driver's seat, throwing the cakes into her handbag. Checking her face in the rear-view mirror, she wipes a smudge of lipstick from her top lip. 'Honestly, that woman.'

'Mum?' I ask as she pulls out into the road. 'Why do you hate Lisa?'

'Not while I'm driving, sweetheart.'

'But Mum, she's nice.'

'Wolf in sheep's clothing, Carmen. Wouldn't want to hang out with her bunch of druggies and losers. Trouble with all that lot is that they didn't know when to call it a day and grow up.'

She brakes suddenly to avoid a car that she's just cut up at the roundabout. I fall forward, the seat belt narrowly saving me from the dashboard. Mum's bags fall off the back seat, things clattering on the floor around my feet.

'Wanker!' she shouts, making a V sign at the back of the car.

Other drivers are beeping their horns. Mum growls and wrenches the gears. 'Oh *piss* off,' she mutters under her breath. She puts her foot violently on the accelerator, jerking the car forwards again. A lipstick rolls under my shoe.

'Anyway,' she says, as she finally gets the car into gear, 'we won't be here much longer. In a couple of years I'll get my promotion. Next stop London. That's where all the *real* people are.'

# 22

Our house is in a new estate in California. Mum thinks this is the best joke ever. 'Just wait till I tell your nan.'

The houses are red, bricks the colour of stewed tea. The white shiny plastic window frames are criss-crossed with fake leading to make them look old-fashioned. The door closes behind us with a suck of air, as if we're being shut inside a Tupperware tub.

The woman showing us round has thick, meaty calves. Walking up the stairs behind her Mum points to them and hisses, 'Look at that – ham on the bone.'

'And here is the front bedroom.' She shows us into the room. It's square and poky with tiny windows that look out over the liquorice curve of the tarmac and the rubble that will become the rest of the estate.

'It's lovely,' Mum says. 'Just what we were looking for.'

We'll be moving in next month. Just in time for Christmas.

I'm making a scrapbook. Cutting out pictures from Mum's magazines. In it I am writing everything I know about being beautiful so that I won't forget what I have to do.

I have two lists: IN and OUT.

On the OUT list it says:

*Split ends.*

*Dirty fingernails.*
*Yellow teeth.*
*Bad breath.*
*Spots.*
*Dry skin.*
*Bad posture.*
*Hairy legs.*
*Hairy face.*
*Hairy armpits.*
*Fat.*

On the IN list it says:
*Shiny hair.*
*Polished nails.*
*White teeth.*
*Fresh breath.*
*Clear skin.*
*Good posture.*
*Shaved legs and armpits.*
*Thin.*
*Thin is in*, I write. *IN.*

The telly's on but she's not watching it. She's twitching, fiddling with her hair, her leg moving like it's on a spring.

'I don't know,' she says. 'I never know if I'm doing the right thing.'

She looks at me. Waiting for me to speak.

'Don't you think I did the right thing? I mean, for my career? I couldn't have stayed with Bri– your father. I couldn't. I know it was an upheaval, but it's been worth it.' She pauses. 'Hasn't it?'

I stare at her. I am going to be thinner and more

beautiful than her. I'm going to really, really piss her off. I bite my lip and shrug.

'Well, say something. Why don't you ever bloody *say* anything?'

I pretend to watch TV. It's a holiday show. The presenter is walking along a tropical beach. Her legs are the colour of smooth peanut butter.

'You know, with the kind of life I've had, I didn't really have any choice. Having you when I did. Most women these days don't have kids until they're my age. I gave up a lot for you.'

I roll my eyes. 'Big deal,' I say.

'What did you say?'

I shrug.

'Don't you get ungrateful on me.' Her voice is wobbling. Go on, cry, I think. Then I'll win. I haven't eaten anything since yesterday and I'm so hungry I could faint. 'You don't know what it's like for me. Responsibility.' She spits. 'Looking after yourself. How would you cope if I left you to fend for yourself? Hmmm? Where would you be without *me*?'

She's standing over me, blocking out the telly. Her cheeks are like razor blades. Her head looks too big for her body.

'I'm going out. If that's OK with you, Miss Mardypants.'

I'm getting more and more light-headed. I can see spots in front of my eyes, pinpricks of light that only get brighter if I close my eyes. I drink a glass of water but it makes me bloated and leaves a metallic taste in my mouth.

There's no food in. We haven't been to the supermarket for weeks. I open the fridge. It's a little Electrolux with a tiny icebox, and it smells funny when I open it. There's some bottles of water and an apple but no milk. I pick out the apple and polish it against my trousers, but when I bite into it, it's sour and has a weird fuzzy texture. It makes me retch. I throw it in the bin, and instead of hitting the bottom with a thud it makes a squelchy noise as it lands.

I put my hand in gingerly in case I touch something slimy. My fingers grasp like one of those grabbing hands at the fair. I can feel the waxy surface of the apple and the wet raw bit where I've taken a bite. Then the bag. It's been there since the day before yesterday. They'll be edible.

I sit on the kitchen floor and carefully rip the bag open. The icing has congealed a little in the middle, I can see where it's dried out in crusty lumps, but I don't care. I eat both pieces of cake in three huge mouthfuls.

Ten minutes later, when I've drunk another glass of water and squeezed a spot in the mirror, I throw it up again.

By midnight she still hasn't come back. I chew gum, which makes me burp but gets rid of the taste in my mouth. I touch the scar on my hand; it's healed up but there's still a faint purple line where the point of the compass dragged across my skin. I run my thumbnail down it, pressing hard to make the line come back raised and livid. My nail makes crescent indents. One even draws a little blood.

# 23

Nail designs decorate the border of the card.

*You are cordially invited to the grand opening of*
*Lisa's Nail File*
*Professional American Nail Design, Manicures,*
*Extensions & Treatments.*
*RSVP*

I run my fingers over the glittery edges. I'll have to
RSVP, go and find her, tell her that I'd love to come.

I look up where to go in Mum's *A-Z*. It's on the other
side of the city, miles away in Handsworth. I rip the pages
out and slip them inside my biology book.

It's much further than it looked on the map. It's misty,
but not raining. I pull the hood of my jacket over my
head and push my hands down in my pockets so the hood
stretches. I weave along the pavement, pulling faces, like
I'm a Ghostface Killer from *Scream*.

Lisa's shop is on an alley just off the Soho Road. It's
not open but I can see her inside, up a ladder, painting.
She's wearing baggy jeans and scruffy shoes and she's got
her hair tied back in a blue-check headscarf. I can hear her
singing along to the radio even out in the street.

'How embarrassing,' she mouths through the glass, taking off her yellow Marigolds before she unlocks the door to let me in. 'You caught me doing a Doris Day impression.'

The shop is bigger than the market stall, two floors joined by a narrow spiral staircase at the back. She's painting the walls lilac with silver on the staircase. She's got streaks of paint on her face.

'What you doing down my way?' she says, smiling. 'The party's not until next week.' She points to her paintbrush. 'I suppose I could do your nails for you if you like. Might be a bit messy though. You going to give me a hand?'

She shows me around. Up the spiral staircase is a little room with a kitchenette and an armchair by the window.

'I can come up here and get away from the world,' she says. 'It's probably a fire hazard, but I don't care.'

She gives me a brush and tells me to take my coat off in case I get paint on it. She looks at my school uniform. 'I never learned anything at school,' she says, giving me a baggy black sweater. 'Put this on over. I don't want to get you into trouble.'

It's warm in the shop, the radio blasting pop music. Lisa chatters on about how she's going to branch out into piercing 'only ears mind' and mehndi now that she's got more space. She shows me her henna kits. 'Just like Madonna.'

There are boxes everywhere. Nail polish in shoes boxes, all marked by their colour. Six boxes marked RED. Five marked PINK. Four marked PURPLE. And an assortment of GREENS, SILVERS, GOLDS and BLUES. They are all different makes and shades. Hard Candy, Maybelline, Max Factor, Chanel, Ruby & Millie, Urban Decay. Some only have a few dregs left in the bottom. 'Never throw anything away,' she says, seeing me holding one bottle up to the light to see what shade of lime green is inside. 'You never know when you'll need it for a colour mix.'

The colours have amazing names. Crushed Peach, Moonlight Shimmer, Baby Pink, Cream Soda Sparkle, Frosted Wine, Cherry Bomb – like sweets but better.

There's suitcases of accessories. Nail rings, jewels, ribbons, silks, gold leaf, transfers, stencils, and a whole box full of acetone tips. In one box are hundreds of tiny gold dangles, moons, stars, palm trees, beetles, seahorses. All no bigger than a fingertip.

'How was half-term?' she asks eventually.

I carefully put the lid back on a box of sequins. 'He cancelled,' I say.

'Your nana told me. Oh, *sweetheart*.'

I can feel tears but I, swallow them. 'I'm all right,' I say. Then it all comes out, how I want to leave Birmingham, how Mum's being a cow.

'She climbs down the ladder. 'Your mum— Oh dear, Carmen. I'm so *sorry*.'

She's brought an old sofa from home for the back of the shop. We perch on the dust covers, steaming mugs of tea in our hands. She tells me that a long time ago, when Billy had a band and the Power House was still open, she and Mum used to go everywhere together. 'She was a star, your mum. We were like twins. I knew what she was thinking before she even said it.' She bites her lip. 'I'm just telling you this so you know that she hasn't always been so . . . so highly strung. It was her diets that did it you know, they turned her, made her paranoid. Ever since we were teenagers she's been funny about her weight, but after she had you she went a bit . . . well, she

162

went on a crash diet. Worse than before. She wasn't eating *anything*. And she started saying all sorts about me that weren't true.' A fat tear escapes and rolls down her cheek. 'I still love her, you know. If only she'd *talk* to me.'

I start to cry too before I can stop myself. 'Hey hey,' she says, taking my cup of tea and putting it on the floor. 'Come here. There's no point in us both getting upset, is there?'

Caught up in her strong arms I can smell paint and perfume and fags. I sob until I think I might throw up.

'I'm sorry,' I say, eventually, realizing that I've made a big snotty mess down the front of her dungarees.

'Don't be sorry. Here.' She gives me a bit of kitchen roll. 'Shall we stop for lunch? I bet you're really hungry after all that work. You're skinny as a whippet.'

Panic comes like a punch, radiating out from my chest.

'I'm not hungry.' I don't want to eat. Eating just makes everything *worse*.

'I'm going to have some. Painting always make me hungry.'

She brings back bags of food from the curry house round the corner. 'Look,' she says, taking the lids off the foil tubs. 'I got naan bread and chickpeas and paneer and bhajis and some chocolate barfi for afters.'

The room is full of a spicy smell that makes my mouth water. I bet it's got loads of calories in it.

'Go on, help yourself.' She hands me a plate. 'Think of all those calories you've used up getting here.' She smiles, her mouth wrinkling at the edges. I can tell she's older than Mum. 'Go on, I won't tell.'

She says that she used to diet all the time like Mum, but she stopped. 'It's a vicious circle. Once you start it's

163

really hard to stop. Better to eat when you're hungry. Don't you think?'

I take a small spoon of everything and tear off a piece of the bread. It's delicious, all different flavours and textures. My belly grumbles loudly.

'See?' Lisa says, hearing it. 'You *were* hungry after all.'

'Why are you looking so pleased with yourself?' Mum asks.

I've come back to find she's getting ready to go out again: 'Just a little drink with the girls from work.'

'I got an A for my homework,' I lie.

'Did you, darling?'

On her way out she kisses me, leaving a greasy smear of lipstick on my forehead.

Watching TV, I think about the food I ate with Lisa and feel bad for not throwing it up. I'll probably put on pounds now. I scratch my arm with the ringpull from my Coke can, drawing lines on my skin, like a game of noughts and crosses. I push deeper, harder, until blood bubbles to the surface. I don't feel a thing.

When she comes back there's someone with her. It's not the same voice as before. Not so deep and gravelly. He makes more noise while he's doing it. AhAhAh-ing as if he's too tender to touch.

He's there in the morning. Sat in the lounge with a cup of tea.

'Sweetheart, this is Bob.'

Bob has sideburns and overgrown hair. He looks like the singer from Oasis.

'Bob's in a band, aren't you, Bob?'

He looks at me vacantly.

'Oose this then?'

'Carmen, my little girl.'

'How old you say you was?' he asks, looking at Mum. 'Sh'aint no toddler, is she?' Then looking at me. 'No offence, darlin', but your mother told us she was twenty-five.'

There's a lot to do to get a shop ready for opening. Even a small one like Lisa's.

'It's got to look nice. People come here to treat themselves. Tender loving customer care,' Lisa says. 'That's what we've lost. I mean I'm not having a go at your mum but those chain shops don't really give a shit. One size fits all, know what I mean?'

The party's tonight and Billy's come round to help. He drops off a few chairs salvaged from the restaurant and puts racks all along one wall for Lisa to put her polish on.

'Your mother coming to the party, then?' Billy asks me.

I look at Lisa, unsure what to say.

'She's got an invitation,' Lisa says.

'Funny, isn't it?' Lisa says as she plugs in the till. 'How we both ended up in retail in the end.'

'Y'what?' Billy asks.

'Me and Maria. After all the fuss.'

They make funny faces at each other. 'The wind will change and you'll get stuck like that,' Billy says in a silly voice.

Lisa sets up her table. A lamp, an airbrush, a pot of tiny paintbrushes, a hot lamp for quick drying, a basket of cotton wool. She puts all her lotions, creams, basecoats, strengtheners and removers in the drawers. She has a toolkit too, a tiny one with awls for piercing nails, clippers, scrapers, orangewood cuticle removers and a tiny nail file. 'Never use a metal file,' she says. 'You only end up splitting the nail. Always use an emery board because you can get them with different grains. Feel that' – she wipes one across the back of my hand, it scratches – 'that one's for filing nails down. 'Whereas this one' – this time it only tickles – 'is for shaping them.'

She puts up her pictures on the wall behind. One is of Annmarie and Patti dressed up for a party, their hair in spiralling coils, their faces painted silver.

'That was in Berlin,' she says, seeing me looking. 'Annmarie used to live over there.'

Above it she pins the picture of Debra. 'That's my girl,' she says to herself, touching it lightly with the tips of her nails.

'I found a picture of your mum,' she says. 'Look, wasn't she gorgeous?'

It doesn't look like Mum. She's got her hair down, falling in thick tresses over her shoulders. Her nails are long and sparkling and she's looking straight at the camera, her face radiant. 'Used to be the life and soul, your mother. But that bit of her packed off on holiday somewhere.' She sighs and pins the photo up, next to Annmarie. 'Maybe she'll come back again, some day.'

When everything looks tidy and she's made me carry all the empty boxes upstairs, she persuades Billy to let her do his nails for the football.

'You're always trying to make me look like a girl,' he moans.

Lisa lowers her eyes and smiles. 'You used to love wearing make-up.'

'Only when I was young and pretty. No one wants to see fat, hairy bastards in slap.'

'It's not slap, it's your *nails*.' Lisa primes her airbrush, releasing a hiss of air. 'Different thing. Come on.'

Billy puts his hands on the table, he has wide nails and long, thick fingers. He sits rigidly, not moving his neck, watching Lisa as she airbrushes his nails blue. When it's dry, she carefully paints white stripes on each fingernail and stencils his thumbnails with BCFC. She finishes off with a coat of clear lacquer.

He asks after Mum, and when I tell him that she's fine, he raises his eyebrows. 'Is that what she says?'

'You better win,' Lisa says, touching his nails to check that they're dry. 'With those nails.'

'Yeah, well, need all the luck we can get this season.'

'Oh, come on, we'll make the playoffs this year.'

'Playoffs schmayoffs,' he says. 'Too early to tell.'

When he's gone off to St Andrew's, she talks about him, starting a long time ago, when she was young and my mother even younger. When Billy played guitar in a band, when everyone was having the time of their lives. 'It'll happen to you one day too,' she says. 'You won't notice because you'll be having so much fun, but you'll look back and realize it was the best time of your life.'

Billy was hot property. He had celebrity friends, the boys from UB40, Dexy's Midnight Runners, The Specials. Everyone wanted a bit of him. She shows me an old photo. Mum and Lisa looking at Billy as if he's the most beautiful thing in the world. Mum's thin, but grinning happily. Billy's holding up a bottle to the camera, his face is red, shiny, his eyes soft, half closed. 'Me and your mum, we loved him,' she says simply. 'I still do. He's a star.'

Lisa's had some display boards made specially to go in

the window. I help her pin up all her designs. She wants them separated into airbrushed and hand-painted. The nails on the airbrushed board she does with stencils, whole sets of them – Festival Nails for Christmas, Halloween, Easter, Fireworks, Independence Day, Thanksgiving, St Patrick's Day, St David's Day, even a set of tiny dragons for St George's Day. Party Nails with dangles, rhinestones, glittery polish, and Urban Girl Nails in animal print and camouflage patterns.

On the handpainted board, each design is unique. Handpainted by Lisa. She's done tiny copies of all the Disney characters and a set of film stars: James Dean, Marilyn Monroe, Humphrey Bogart, Lauren Bacall. And a set of nails with Princess Diana on.

'Did those the week before she died,' she says. 'Customer never came back to get them either. Spooky, isn't it?'

My favourites are the abstract airbrush designs. Fiery swirls and glittery squiggles, blue stars and red hearts.

'Can I have my nails like that?'

'You learn to keep up with what you've got first,' she says. 'You don't want to be doing with extensions at your age. Patience. That's what nails are about. Learning to do things slowly. Step by step.'

She surveys the shop, hands on her hips, and asks me if I think it looks ready for a party. I tell her it looks like a cave full of treasure.

She smiles. 'Magpie's nest, more like.'

'No.' she says. 'I said NO, you're *not* going.'

She rubs her hands down the front of her new leather pencil skirt.

'Can't stop me,' I say, trying to dodge past her.

'I can call the police.' She glares at me and stands in front of the door. 'Don't push me because I'll do it. I'll tell them I can't handle you.'

Wish you would, I think. Then I'd be able to do what I liked.

'I'm not having you hanging out with that crowd. You're too young. Billy's all right, but the rest of them are a waste of space. Going nowhere with their lives. Rock and roll is a *look*, Carmen, not a way of life.'

She won't go to bed. She stays up listening to a Paul Oakenfold mix CD dead loud. I look at my face in my compact mirror, use a kohl stick that I nicked from her make-up bag to draw dark lines under my eyes. I use so much that it smudges, but I don't care. I hate my face. I wish I could slice it off.

Annmarie is Lisa's first official customer. She's having her extensions wrapped with gold silk, ribbons, jewels. The full Five Star at a fiver a nail. Fifty quid for all ten nails.

'Hiya, Carmen.' Annmarie kisses the air around my face. 'Bit of an emergency really, Lees, I popped one,' she says, holding up a clear plastic bag with one pink nail in it. 'Feels like I've got a broken tooth.' Lisa smiles and mutters to herself while she holds Annmarie's finger and tries to fit a new nail over the top. 'Looks great in here, Lees, honestly it does. Amazing.' She looks at me. 'How was your party then? You knock 'em dead?'

I shrug. ''S all right.'

'Your party was a right laugh, Lees. Mind if I smoke?'

She fidgets, smoothing her skirt down, twisting round, trying to look out of the window behind her. If Lisa wasn't holding her still by her finger I expect she'd just float straight out of the door.

'Carmen love, make us some tea, there's a darling.'

I climb the stairs to the kitchenette and stare out of the window for ages at the dusty windows of the warehouse opposite. There are binbags of rubbish and empty bottles left over from the party. Even the remains of a Good Luck cake on the side, half eaten. Lisa and Annmarie are laughing downstairs, cackling and coughing, interrupted by big spluttering hoots. I'm sick of being fourteen.

'You know what?' Annmarie says later when I have negotiated two trips down the spiral stairs without spilling any tea. 'You'd look good with short hair you would.'

'Annmarie's a hairdresser,' Lisa says.

I look doubtfully at her nails.

'No, honest,' Annmarie says. 'With nails like mine you just have to learn to use your fingers. A neat little pageboy cut would look a treat on you, you know.'

Then the salon is quiet apart from the radio, reggae classics on PCM. I practise a flower design on a pink base with a violet tip. I paint the flowers in red and leaf green. I try to remember to wipe the brush on the neck of the bottle like Lisa showed me so the paint doesn't blob.

Lisa covers all of Annmarie's nails with a square of gold silk, cutting round the rough edges with a little art blade. 'Don't sneeze, Annmarie, else I'll stab you.' Annmarie purses her lips and watches Lisa. When, finally, each nail is wrapped, Annmarie has to sit still and wait for the glue to dry. 'Light a fag for us, Lees,' she says, pointing to her silver handbag. 'There's a holder in the bottom there somewhere.' Lisa pulls out a long black cigarette holder and fixes a cigarette in the end. Annmarie holds it between her first two fingers, wedged right at the bottom almost between her knuckles.

Annmarie looks at her hands proudly. 'Expensive hobby,' she says, 'but I don't know where I'd be without them. I think I was probably a princess in a former life, but all my riches and jewels got squandered away over time and so I have to have my nails done to remind me of what I once was. What I could have been. When I die, Lisa, I want you to do my nails.'

'What, in your coffin?' Lisa turns up her nose. 'Eugh, don't know if I could.'

'So when archaeologists dig me up, they'll find my nails and they'll put them in a museum. Your work should be in a gallery I tell ya, Lees, it's *amazing*.'

Lisa blushes. 'Oh, shush.'

When Lisa's finished, Annmarie's nails are curling gold talons, wrapped with red ribbons and decorated with tiny clusters of red and blue rhinestones. They're beautiful. On one nail there's a little Chinese dragon transfer, on another a scorpion.

'My lucky signs,' she says. 'Scorpio and Year of the Dragon, that's me. Breathing fire with a sting in her tail.'

'Can I have some pocket money?'

She looks at me. 'What for?'

'I want a haircut.'

She narrows her eyes. 'Nothing wrong with your hair. If you plaited it more often it wouldn't get so tangled. Anyway, you're costing me enough already, young lady.'

The phone rings while she's out. In the middle of *East-Enders*. I ignore it but it goes on for ages.

'Hello? Can I speak to Maria Wiley please?'

I recognize the voice. It's Miss Burton from school.

'Wrong number,' I say, slamming the phone down.

It rings back again but I unplug the phone from the wall.

In the bathroom mirror my hair looks bushy, frizzy, full of split ends. When I was younger Mum used to wash it for me at weekends: rubbing conditioner into my scalp, brushing out all the tangles. There would always be a big bird's nest of hairs left in the hairbrush at the end. 'You've got beautiful hair,' she'd say when she was done, and my hair fell flat against my head, the hairs straightened and smoothed.

I get the kitchen scissors, the ones with orange handles and cut off a wedge of hair just under my ear. Once I've started I have to carry on, but it's hard to cut at the back so I have to guess and when I look in the mirror it's just horrible. All different lengths, some long bits still straggling over my shoulders. I cut even more. Just chopping now, randomly hacking off clumps until it's really short all over. It looks mad.

I use handfuls of the Brylcreem that appeared in the bathroom the morning after one of her nights out and rub big jelly blobs of it in, making clumps of hair stick up at funny angles.

It would look good if it was blue.

# 24

'What the *hell* have you done?' She puts her hand in front of her face. 'You can't go to school like that.'

She stalks around the living room. I sip my cup of black tea. She can't touch me. She can't.

'Look at you. You look ridiculous. *Ridiculous.*' She's shaking with anger. 'You're too fat in the face to carry that off. You look . . .' her face twists, '. . . like a baby.'

'So?' I say.

She slaps me across the face, once, twice, until I spill my tea trying to avoid her. I push her away from me so she staggers and falls back into the armchair. I grab my bag, put my coat on and pull the hood up.

'Where are you going?'

'To school,' I mumble, remembering to slam the door behind me.

I run and run down the corridor, my shoes squeaking against the tiles. When I get to the lifts I can hear her shouting my name down the corridor. 'Carmen! Come back here!' But I ignore her and start running down the stairs before she can get me.

Outside, it's raining again, drizzling and grey. I pull my hood round my face, tying the toggles under my chin and run towards the road that will take me to Lisa's shop. The air in the soles of my Nike Air Max make it feel like

I'm running on springs, like I could run for ever, my feet pounding the tarmac. I run right through town and out again, ducking down alleyways through underpasses, right across Centenary Square and over the bridge to Hockley, through the crowds of suits scurrying to work. When I get to the Soho Road I have to stop. The wind is up, sending soggy leaves flying in little eddies of air. I am damp, steaming, desperate for breath. My legs are trembling, my chest hurts. When I wipe my sleeve across my face to dry it, I realize I am crying.

'Oh, my God, Carmen. What happened to you?' The shop is muggy. Lisa's got her electric heater on. There's an older woman in, having a manicure and a French polish. 'What happened to your hair?'

'I cut it,' I say.

'Looks like you had a fight with some hedgeclippers,' the old woman says. 'Why aren't you at school?'

'It's all right, Mrs Denby. It's my niece. She's got the day off today. Why don't you go upstairs for a bit, Carmen? Dry yourself off. I'll be up in a minute when I've done this. Put the kettle on, pet.'

When she comes upstairs she won't look me in the eye. She asks me if Mum cut my hair. 'You can tell me the truth, you know.'

I tell her it was me. All by myself. 'I hate my hair,' I say.

She touches it, lifting tufts of it up and letting them drop. 'I've got some clippers downstairs. Why don't you let me tidy it up for you?'

It tickles as she runs the buzzing clippers over my scalp. She tells me that when she was my age she shaved her eyebrows off, just to see what it looked like. 'It was a mess,' she says. 'I looked the same as before, I just had no eyebrows.'

When she's finished it's really, really short. I can see my white skin through the bristles of hair. Almost a number one. She's left me a fringe at the front that flops down over my forehead. 'Proper little feather cut,' she says, and starts plaiting my fringe into tiny plaits.

It looks quite cool. She fixes little painted beads on the end of each plait.

'There,' she says. 'Warrior princess. Let me just do your eyebrows to match. Sit still.'

She uses narrow wax strips to make my eyebrows a nice neat shape. It hurts when she rips them off.

'*Aww.*'

'Sorry, sweetheart. Stings a bit, doesn't it?' When she's finished she gives me a mirror. 'You look lovely,' she says.

My face is different, sharper. When I frown, my eyebrows come closer together, making me look spiky, mean.


She's not in but there's a brand-new exercise bike in the lounge, still in its plastic wrapping.

'Oooh, I always loved the view from here,' Lisa says, rushing to the window. 'Used to love coming here to visit Billy.'

She insisted on coming back with me. 'I want to have a word with your mother,' she said. She shut up the shop early and everything. All the way back on the bus I've been dreading it. Mum is going to go mental, I know she is.

Lisa noses around the flat. 'Doesn't she keep any food in?' she asks, opening the fridge. 'There isn't even any milk.'

'We're moving next week,' I say, suddenly embarrassed. 'No point in shopping before we move.'

'Who says? You or your mother?' She looks at me. 'Look, Carmen. This can't carry on, sweetheart,' she says. 'We're worried about you. You've got to tell us if there's something wrong. Me and Billy we care about you. If—' she clears her throat, 'if your mother—' but she doesn't finish her sentence. A man in blue overalls comes crashing through the door followed by Mum. He's carrying a bench press.

'Just put it there,' Mum says, pointing to the space next to the exercise bike. She looks at me and Lisa and gives me one of her I'll-deal-with-you-later looks.

'What are you doing here? Ganging up on me? Might have known her strange haircuts had something to do with you. It's really quite inconvenient. I'm got a delivery to take care of.'

'It's all right,' Lisa says, sitting down, 'I can wait.'

My mother reminds Lisa that I am her daughter and she will bring me up how she sees fit. 'She has to learn about the world, Lisa. It's cruel out there when you've not got looks. She's got to learn to make the best of what she's got.'

Mum has sent me to my room but I can hear what they're saying because I've pulled the door open a crack. Outside it's really windy, air howling through the gaps around the windows, blowing in great gusts against the side of the tower, making it shudder.

'She's not going to school, Maria, she's been hanging around my shop.'

That's not *fair*. She told me I could come round the

shop. I want to shout something, but I bite my lip so hard I can taste blood.

'You should have phoned me if she's been making a nuisance of herself.'

'She's not. I'm just worried about her. She looks too thin.' There's a pause, the sound of Mum's lighter flicking. 'So do you.'

'Lisa's got no right interfering,' she says. Standing in the doorway, in silhouette she looks like a bird, all claws and bone. She goes on about how humiliated she is. How I've betrayed her. 'I won't have you sneaking around behind my back. Telling tales. There will no more *sneaking*, Carmen. And now we've got a home gym you can get into more of a routine.'

She uses the exercise bike later. I can hear the buzz of the wheels spinning uselessly as she pedals against air. She puts on her *Ibiza Anthems* CD. She doesn't get off until she's listened to it twice.

She comes on the bus with me to school the next day. Walks me right up to the gates. 'God knows what they'll say about your hair,' she says, rolling her eyes.

Miss Burton makes me stay behind after class. 'Is everything all right at home, Carmen? I tried your number the other day but somebody told me I'd got the wrong number. Have you moved?'

'Yes, Miss,' I say.

'And your hair. I must say it's quite a surprising look. You know it's against school regulations, don't you?'

'Yes, Miss.'

'You know I'm going to have to contact your parents about this?'

177

'Yes, Miss.'

'Perhaps you'd like to give me your new number?'

I give her Dad's mobile number.

I see them after break outside the canteen. Kelly is standing with them. At least, I think it's Kelly. She looks different. She's got no glasses on and she's had her braces taken off. Her hair is shorter and clipped back with pink slides.

'Look who's back,' Maxine says.

'What happened to your hair?' Paisley says. 'Are you trying to be cool or something? Because you look *weird*.'

'Like a lezzie,' Maxine hisses.

'Weirdo,' Kelly says. She's even learned to curl her lip like them.

I hiss at them, baring my teeth.

They huddle together, pretending to be scared.

'Oooh, I think it farted,' Paisley says. They all fall about laughing.

I run at them screaming, punching Paisley and scratching Kelly on the face.

'Piss OFF! *Piss off.*'

Other girls have to pull me off, hold me back. The chant goes round the canteen. *Fight, fight, fight.* Kelly balls her hand into a fist and lands one on my mouth. I can hear my lip ripping. Warm blood dribbles down my chin. I suck it into my mouth, swill it round with my saliva and spit it back in her face. It lands on her neck, a dark shiny blob of it. Before she can retaliate, Miss Burton comes round the corner to break us up, her face red and thunderous.

Mum tugs her skirt down over her thighs nervously.

'I can't believe I'm here,' she says. 'Makes me feel like a schoolgirl.' We're sitting in the waiting room outside the headmistress's office. One of the school secretaries makes Mum a cup of tea which she leaves undrunk under her chair because it's got full-fat milk in it.

The headmistress talks to Mum like she's a child. 'Not sending your child to school is a serious offence in the eyes of the law, Mrs Wiley. Carmen is already behind with her schoolwork and is going to struggle to catch up.'

'We're aware there have been family difficulties, Mrs Wiley,' Miss Burton says. She's loving this, I can tell, nosing into other people's business. She doesn't look like she's got much of a life of her own. Sour old slapper. 'We've already spoken to your, er, to Carmen's father, about this. It's not our policy to interfere with your personal life, Mrs Wiley, but we are quite concerned about Carmen's welfare.'

Mum's eyes narrow to slits and for a moment I think she's going to freak out. But she tries another tactic. 'I know,' she says. 'It's all my fault. But we've made a bit of a promise, haven't we, Carmen, to try and get along a bit better?'

'Er, yes,' I say.

'Now, Mrs Wiley,' says the headmistress, 'there's no need to feel you must take all the blame. Like I said we're here to help.'

'Help,' echoes Miss Burton, nodding vigorously. She's loving this, nosy bitch. She looks at me. 'We do understand,' she says. 'Teenagers can be difficult.'

They're trying to turn Mum against me. I grab her hand and she lifts herself from her twisted position – legs crossed, arms crossed, elbows resting on her knees, as if she's trying hard to keep herself upright.

'I'm not sorry,' I say, 'they were provoking me.'

Miss Burton and the headmistress look at each other.

'Well, next time perhaps you should take a deep breath and count to twenty,' Miss Burton says.

They talk about fresh starts and clean slates. Mum gazes out of the window distractedly, while they tell me that I will have to make an effort to catch up and that I will be on report until the Christmas holidays. 'A doctor's note must be provided for any absences. Do you understand?'

'Yes,' we say in unison.


'I'm a bad mother to you, Carmen,' she says, lying on the couch looking at the exercise bike. She says she's too tired to get on it tonight.

I don't say anything, because I know that it's true. I know that other people have nice mothers, mothers like Lisa.

'Next week, when we move house, can we start again?'

'OK,' I say.

She starts crying, quietly and then louder, until she's sobbing, her whole body shaking. 'I'm terrible at everything,' she says. 'I never should have brought you here.'

Then she goes quiet. Curling herself into a little ball, tucking her hands around her head and staring through the exercise bike at the blank TV screen.

'Mum? Are you OK?'

Her eyelids flutter as if she is just about to fall asleep. 'Mmmm?'

'Are you OK?'

'I'm fine, sweetheart, just fine.' She sounds far away, like she's on the end of a long-distance phone call.

'Can I get you anything?'

'No, sweetheart, you go to bed. I'll stay here and watch a bit of telly.'

'But it's not on.'

'What?'

'The telly. D'you want me to put it on?'

'No no, you're all right. You just go to bed.'

When I get up in the morning she's still lying there, staring at the blank TV screen, eyes wide open.

Dad calls. 'I got a call from school. Is everything all right, love?'

I tell him that everything's fine, that we're moving into a new house next week. I try to sound cheerful, happy. Mum watches me while I talk to him, wiping her eyes with toilet roll.

He says he might come down and give us a hand with our moving. That he's pleased Mum's doing so well. 'Sounds like she's really pulling it together down there,' he says. 'I'm impressed.'

'I miss you,' I say, before I can stop myself. I sound like a right sap.

'You too, sugarpuff,' he says, but his voice is distracted, far away. I'm embarrassed. I know he's only saying it. He's not even my real dad.

He rings again after the weekend to say he's sorry he can't get down. Too much on at work.

'See?' Mum says, when I tell her. 'See what we're up against?'

I go to school. Turn up every morning at eight-thirty with my form for the headmistress. Paisley and Maxine and Kelly call me names when they see me. I ignore them.

I eat apples for lunch and drink chocolate milk that I throw up later, before the bell for registration.

I sit at the back of class and don't answer any questions. I write *Fuck* on the cover of my maths book, and *Everybody's Weird* when we're supposed to be doing fractions. It's the human body in biology: I missed the heart, the lungs and the liver. They're doing the skeleton and the nervous system now. Miss Burton shows me the thick wedge of textbook pages that I've missed.

She gives me some question-and-answer sheets. 'I'm so pleased we've been able to sort all this out,' she says. 'I'm sure things will settle down for you soon.'

Lisa offers me a manicure. Black with silvery rhinestones on each nail.

''S all right,' I say, 'I can do my own now.'

'I *had* to tell her, Carmen. She's your mother and you don't want Social Services getting involved.'

'Better than school,' I say.

'No, Carmen, it's not.' She sounds irritated. 'Once Social Services get involved you never know where you'll end up. I'm family and I care about you.'

Yeah, right. Wanted rid of me more like.

'I didn't want to be a nuisance,' I say.

'Oh, sweetheart.' She lifts my chin with her hands, makes me look her in the eye. 'You're not a nuisance. I love having you around the place. It's just that you've got to go to school. It's the law. Sod's law maybe, but still the law. Do you want to end up in a home?'

I shake my head.

'You can still come and hang out on Saturdays and after school if you like.'

*'Really?'*
'Really.'
I offer her my hands.

# 25

Billy comes over in the Steers van. I help him load up while Mum packs our boxes and suitcases. We have to dodge between showers; the rain has been heavy since first thing. There isn't much to take. The exercise bike and the bench press are the only bits of furniture we've got. Everything else belongs to Billy.

It's the same van he used for Lisa's shop. There are flecks of glitter on the floor from one of Lisa's packets that split.

'Can't get rid of the bloody stuff. Everywhere I go I keep finding bits of it stuck to me.' He raises his eyebrows. 'You women and your bloody sparkles,' he says.

I flash my nails at him. 'Exactly,' he says. 'Bloody sparkles.' Then, as if he's worried about offending me, 'Looks good on you, though.'

There's Asda bags in the back full of food. Frozen pizzas, milk, marg, eggs, fruit and veg, tea bags, toilet rolls even a strip of KitKats.

'Lisa went shopping yesterday,' he says. 'But don't tell your mum. I'll pretend it was me, else she'll throw it away. You know what she's like.'

Mum is paranoid about forgetting stuff. 'Honestly, at the moment I'd forget my head if it wasn't screwed on.' She has to go back upstairs to doublecheck three times before she'll let Billy drive off, even though he has told her she can fetch anything she's forgotten whenever she likes.

'There's no one else moving in, you can hang on to the keys as long as you need to,' he reassures her.

The third time she comes down with an earring. A silver teardrop that Dad gave her for Christmas. 'See?' she says, showing it to us. 'I would have been upset if I'd lost that.'

Billy puts music on in the van – *The Buzzcocks Greatest Hits* – he sings along like a howling dog.

*'What do I get? I don't get yooooou.'*

'Do we have to listen to this?' Mum says, covering her hands with her ears.

'You used to love it,' Billy says, turning it down a fraction, tapping his ring on the steering wheel. 'All that ravey-davey rubbish you listen to now, it's spoiled proper music.'

'At least it's got a melody.'

*'And your mother wants to know what all those stains are on your jeans, You're an orgasm addi—'*

'For God's sake, Billy,' Mum says, leaning forward and pressing the tape out of the machine. 'We're not teenagers any more.'

'Aren't we?' Billy asks arching his eyebrows and looking at her from the corner of his eye. 'I'd give anything to be Carmen's age again.'

When we get to the new house she tries to pick up her box of diet books but it's too heavy. She staggers a little, holding her head.

'Steady there, Maria.'

185

'Don't talk to me like that,' she says, suddenly angry. 'Don't take the piss.'

Billy ignores her and goes inside.

'Mum, he's only being nice.'

She rubs a hand across her forehead fiercely. 'I don't know what's wrong with me,' she says, almost mumbling. 'You got any mints, love? Polos or something?'

'I'll ask Billy.'

He's staring out of the window. 'Mum says she needs some sugar,' I say, 'I'm sorry.'

'Once a selfish cow, always a selfish cow.' He says. 'I know she's your mother, but sometimes—' he fishes half a packet of Extra Strong Mints out of his pocket. 'Tell her not to eat them all at once.'

The house makes me sneeze. When Mum puts the heating on the air becomes thick with dust and the smell of new carpets.

Billy has already broken into the shopping, helping himself to some KitKats and a few slices of bread and marg. There is nothing in the lounge apart from the TV, a few boxes and Mum's exercise equipment. She has ordered a new suite on five years' interest-free credit – 'You'll have left home by the time I have to pay it back' – but they're not delivering until tomorrow.

'It'll be nice when you've got a few bits to go round,' Billy says. 'Snug as bugs. Place heats up lovely.'

It is already getting dark. The builders' lorries roar and sound their horns. Hammering, muffled by the double glazing, has been going on all day. The other houses won't be ready until after Christmas. Out the back of ours there's a freshly turfed lawn, a cleanly creosoted fence and a brand-new whirligig washing line.

When Billy's gone she looks at the bags of shopping. 'He needn't have bought all that,' she says. 'What did he do that for?' She picks out the strip of KitKats and bites her lip, looking at me coyly. 'I suppose we could treat ourselves, couldn't we?'

Her hands shake while she pours the water for tea. Some of it spills in hot splashes on to the side. 'Oh, my dear, my nerves,' she says.

She breaks a KitKat in half, gives me one half, puts the other by her mug.

She eats it crumb by crumb, breaking off tiny pieces of chocolate and wafer with her nails. She sucks each piece, closing her eyes while she does. 'Mmm,' she says, 'aren't I a pig?'

I don't eat mine to see what she will do, leaving it on the arm of the chair. She notices straight away. 'Don't you want yours?'

I shrug. 'Not hungry.'

'Oh.'

When I look again, it's gone, she's got her mouth full of chocolate. When she sees me looking she nearly chokes. She spits it out into a tissue, chocolate dribbling down her chin.

'I just wanted the taste of it in my mouth,' she says.

Later she bins all the food that Billy brought over, only keeping the coffee and tea. 'There's no point in keeping it in. It will only throw us off track.'

Nana turns up in a taxi.

'Oooh, isn't it airy?' she says, opening all the doors. 'Aren't you doing well for yourself?'

She touches my hair. 'All the rage now, is it?' she asks. 'Our Lisa used to have her hair like that.' I stroke my hair, it's not as spiky as it was now it's started growing back.

'Looks like a toilet brush,' Mum says. 'Lisa has a lot to answer for, putting ideas in her head.'

Nana gives us a box of Roses. 'A housewarming present,' she says. 'I know it's not much.'

Mum puts them down the side of the sofa, hides them under a cushion without even saying thank you.

I eat like a machine. I can put two in my mouth at once and swallow them almost whole. The house is too hot, sneezy. I can't taste the chocolate, only the new carpets, the paint fumes. It takes ten minutes to eat the whole box, including the ones with hard centres.

The bathroom is right next to Mum's room. I run the tap full on so the water squeals and I try not to retch too loudly. I am getting good at this. The box of Roses slides back up, silently, obediently.

She's bought a new picture for the lounge. A huge framed print. *The Bridge*, by Salvador Dali. It's a weird, mustard-yellow colour, a desert landscape full of wreckage, a bridge to nowhere in the middle. Walking over the bridge are thin, skeletal figures; sad-looking women draped in blue cloth. As they walk higher their shapes get thinner, more shadowy, until they are just pale outlines floating up into the sky.

Mum looks at it when she's hung it, just behind the TV, so big that it takes up nearly the whole wall. 'That's what I want to be like,' she says, touching one of the figures. 'Made of air.'

# 26

Victoria is stopping the night. Mum's made me do up my bed. Sheets fresh out of the packet, knife-edge creases in them. She's sending me round to Nana's for the night in a taxi, but it's late and Victoria has arrived first. 'Oh, Victoria, *lovely* to see you,' Mum says when she arrives. 'Carmen was just leaving.'

I sit on the uncomfortable new DFS sofa bundled up in my bench coat while they twitter in the kitchen over their fruit teas. Ginseng and vanilla with two tabs of Candarel. I pull my hood up so Victoria won't say anything about my hair.

'Hello,' she says, standing awkwardly in the lounge doorway, her eyes not meeting mine.

I nod at her, pretend to be reading Mum's *OK!* magazine.

She gets on the exercise bike, turns a few cycles. 'Your mum use this often then?' she asks.

'Three times a day,' I say.

Her mouth makes a little O and she starts cycling a bit faster, kicking off her shoes to get a better grip on the pedals. 'I usually do four,' she boasts. The bones in her hips are jutting out of her trousers, her joints click against each other.

After a few minutes, she stops abruptly, folds her arms

over the handlebars and hangs her head. 'Oh,' she says, gasping for breath. 'Oh, would you just get me some water?'

As I stand up, the doorbell goes. 'Sorry,' I say, 'got a taxi waiting.'

On the way to Nana's the driver goes really fast, bombing down the dual carriageway. He doesn't talk to me, though I can see him watching me in his rear-view mirror. I wish this drive would never stop, just go on and on and on, carry me off somewhere, anywhere, different from here.

Nana's watching *Blind Date*. She loves Cilla. 'Had her type at the Butlins,' she says. 'Voices like tannoys, all flat and booming, but everybody loved them because they did all the songs.'

I don't take my coat off and sink into the sofa, even though with Nana's gas fire on full blast it's suffocatingly hot.

She's had the council round again she says, about the hedge. 'They're going to fine your Grandad thousands if he doesn't get rid of it, but he won't listen to me.' He runs off down the pub, she never talks to him these days. 'You know,' she says, 'I've been thinking I might get a divorce. Why should I bother sticking with him now? What do I get? No one comes to visit any more.'

Even though I am sitting behind her I can see her shoulders are twitching. She sniffs. 'There's a packet of Gypsy Creams on the side in the kitchen. Bring them in for us will you, love?'

Halfway through the Lottery programme the doorbell goes. Nana's sat with her tickets clutched in her hand. Ten pound a week she spends on them. She says the first thing she's going to do if she wins is pay someone to cut the hedge down.

'Get that will you? If it's the Jehovah's Witnesses tell them we're heathens.'

When I open the door it's two men, one much younger than the other. Father and son, I reckon. They look like each other, same ears and smarmy, menacing smiles.

'It's Next Door,' the older one says, 'come round about the hedge. Are you alone? Only we wanted to speak to your grandparents. About the hedge.'

'There's no one in,' I lie.

They grunt. 'You sure?' They look past me suspiciously. Next week they say, next week they're going to chop it all down and send us the bill. It's driving everyone round here nuts. They've even written to the telly about it.

When I tell Nana who it was and what they wanted she sighs.

'At least if it went on the telly that would be something to look forward to.'


I'm in bed by the time Grandad gets in, but I can hear them arguing in the front room.

'He's a pervert, next door. I've heard things about him, Joyce.'

'*Rubbish*,' she spits. 'Pub gossip, Ray, no more no less. No reason to keep the house in darkness is it? I *told* you that stuff grew faster than you could cut it. But would you listen?'

Grandad mumbles something and Nana snorts. 'Please yourself,' she says. 'But don't expect me to back you up when they get an injunction out on you.'

In the morning they're not talking to each other. Grandad pretends to read the paper and Nana huffs while she makes breakfast. She gets narky at me when I will only eat the tinned tomatoes on my plate.

'Since when have you been as fussy as your mother?'

The polish is nearly all gone now. I sit in maths chipping off the last little flecks of black. I picked the rhinestones off ages ago. Nana's house has stuck to my clothes; the stale fags and frying seems to have soaked in to my skin, my hair.

There's something going on with Maxine. She's not been at school all week. Paisley put a note in my hand this morning. *Hiya Carmen, I don't hate you any more and I know you're not a lezzie.* She keeps turning round to catch my eye. I pretend not to look.

I meet her in the toilets at break. She pushes me into a cubicle and for a moment my heart sinks. This was a trap, I think. I'm going to get my head kicked in.

'No, no, shhhh,' Paisley says, as I start to struggle. 'I'm not gonna hurt you, *honest.*'

'Well what then?' I ask, impatient.

She starts talking really fast. 'It's Maxine. Dean took some pictures of her and he's put them on the Internet, look.'

She takes a crumpled piece of paper from her pocket. It's a printout of a webpage. In the centre is Maxine, naked, blowing a kiss at the camera; you can see her fanny and everything.

'All the boys at Camp Hill are talking about it.'

Underneath it there's a caption that reads *Teen slut is always up for it.* I'm glad it's not me, I think, cringing at the thought of people seeing me like that, my belly, my tits.

'There's worse pictures than this,' Paisley says, her eyes wide. 'There's pictures of them *doing* it.'

*'Really?'*

She tells me that Maxine will probably leave school. That her parents have got the police in. 'They're gonna get Dean for underage sex.'

I push her hand away. I don't want to look at Maxine any more, pouting stupidly at Dean behind the camera.

Paisley says she's worried that her mum is threatening to take her out of school and teach her at home. 'After the party and everything.' She puts the picture of Maxine back in her pocket, smiles at me nervously. 'I don't mind about Carter. We've finished now. He was only an interim relationship.'

When I ask her how she knows this, she says she read it in *Cosmo*. 'Interim relationships, they're like relationships that you have when you're waiting for something else. You can have him if you like.'

'Never wanted him,' I say. 'He wanted *me*.'


It's dark when school finishes. The leaves have all fallen off the trees making the pavements a soggy, slippery mush. I get the number eleven from school but it takes nearly an hour to run the whole circle round to Handsworth.

There are no lights on. It says on the door that she's open until five and then underneath it gives a mobile number for emergencies. I bang on the door in case she's upstairs but no one comes. I want to tell her about Maxine and Dean.

I scribble her a note on the back of an empty fag packet.

*Dear Lisa, Where are you?!!! Came to see you but you weren't here. Give us a ring. Carmen*

And I post it through the letter box.

I have to push the door hard because it sticks already.

'Happens in all new houses,' Mum had said, sounding like the builders' brochure. 'The building takes a while to *settle*.' As if it was a dog, folded up in its basket, twitching before it sleeps.

The house is dark, though I know she's in because her bags are by the door. The central heating is on full blast, and I'm sweating after the cold outside.

'Mum?'

I go upstairs. Her door is closed, but when I knock on it she moans.

She looks like she did when she was sick, when they hooked her up to so many drips and machines she had to have a room all to herself.

I ask her if anyone's called.

'Why? You got a boyfriend?'

She says she's feeling a bit under the weather, rolling over on her side to look at me. Her eyes bulge as her skin pulls taut, the pressure making them stick out.

'You all right, Mum?'

She sighs heavily. 'I'm just a bit tired, sweetheart.'

There are tissues crumpled up on the floor by the bed. I think she's been crying. I sit on the bed next to her, put my hand on the slope of her hip. She winces.

'Don't touch me, sweetheart.' She takes my hand and presses my knuckles with her fingers. 'Are you OK?'

I nod. 'Yeah.'

She's left her cigarettes on the arm of the sofa. She only

194

has six left. Watching the news, I smoke them all, one after the other, until I feel sick.

Lisa doesn't ring. I reckon she must be tired of me by now. I empty the matches out of the box and light them one after the other, until there's a pile like a bonfire in the ashtray. I roll up some bits of tissue and put them underneath and with the last match set it alight.

The noise is piercing. An endless *beepbeepbeep* that tears through the house. Mum stands in the doorway, her hands covering her ears. 'Switch it off!' she's shouting. 'Switch it off. Switch it off.' She moves anxiously from foot to foot like a clockwork toy. I don't want to look at her too hard. I can see her jawline, the muscles in her cheeks, her huge head. She looks like a lollypop.

'I don't know what to do,' I say.

She points to the smoke alarm blinking on the ceiling. 'Take the battery out,' she shouts.

When it's done, she goes on at me for smoking, but not really very loudly. She's grey and shrivelled, like she's old. Really, really old, like, almost dead.

'You know once,' she says, slowly and thickly, like her tongue is swollen up. 'Men used to fall over themselves for me.'

She shakes her head. 'And now I'm all on my *own*.' She starts to cry.

*But you've got me*, I want to say, *you're not on your own*. But I don't because I know that really, I am not what she wants.

Sealed into my room, I don't sleep. I leave the curtains open and lie at the foot of my bed so I can see the moon and the stars; I miss the view from the flat, the sound of the wind, the endless view. Here, the sky seems too close, like it's pressing down on us.

I don't know if I'm awake or dreaming when I see her, pale as a ghost, standing next to the bed. I close my eyes tight.

# 27

'I came to see you,' I say, 'you weren't here. I left a note.'

Lisa looks up at me. 'I didn't get it, sweetheart. What was it about?'

I shrug. I don't want to talk about it now. I'll just sound like a sap, like I'm trying to get her attention or something. 'It's all right now,' I say.

'Is it?' she asks. 'Just one of those things?'

'Yeah.'

A blob too much green paint drips off the brush on to the nail, making the fish I've been doing misshapen. I'm copying an aquarium design, like the one in Lisa's *Nails* magazine. I've already done a thumbnail with a seahorse on it, but I can't get the index nail right. It's supposed to be an angelfish swimming through seaweed, only it looks like a blob swimming through other blobs. I sigh and flip the nail across the room.

'Watch it,' Lisa says, sounding annoyed. I'm bugging her, I can tell. I bet she really doesn't want me here right now. 'Try the Christmas design, it's easier,' she says.

The Christmas design is holly with red berries on a plum-pudding coloured background. A basecoat, a coat of Plum Pudding, followed by the holly stencil, filled in green and then the red holly stencil for the berries. It doesn't look as good as it does with an airbrush, but when

I've done one I stick it on the board anyway. 'Goes down well at office parties that one,' Lisa says.

'What you doing at Christmas?' she asks later, when there aren't any customers in and we're having tea together. 'Only another couple of weeks to go and all. I can't believe it. It's all come about so quick.'

'Going round Nana's.'

'Are you now?' Lisa laughs. 'What time?'

I shrug. 'For lunch.'

'See you there then.'

'Does Mum know?' I ask.

Lisa shakes her head. 'It's time me and your mother made up, don't you think?'

Mum says the Christmas rush has started for real. She isn't getting back until eight or nine now. 'It's like a war zone out there.'

And there's still over two weeks to go.

I'm doing a set of silver hearts on a pink background on Lisa's acetone tips. It looks all right apart from one where I put too much silver paint in the stencil and it blots. I draw some designs out on a bit of paper, swirls and leaves and yin-yang signs. I want to do something supercool for Lisa. Something she won't have seen before, but I can't really think of anything.

I rub off the olive-green camouflage that Lisa put on yesterday, using cheap Constance Carol remover that is so strong it makes my eyes water, and put on a coat of Golden Shimmer instead. I sit really still with my hands on my knees waiting for it to dry.

When Mum comes in, she opens a packet of ready salted crisps. 'Have you eaten, Carmen?' she asks. 'Only I can't be bothered with cooking. I'm not really hungry.'

198

She's lying, because she never cooks.

She eats a couple of crisps then offers me the bag, but I refuse, showing her my nails. 'No?' She crumples the bag. 'I'm not that hungry anyway.' She throws the crisps in the bin, turns the tap on, pours a glass of water.

'Theresa said one of the customers complained that I was too thin.'

She stands at the doorway, her hand on her hipbone. She seems to sag, like someone's taken all the air out of her. Her laugh is hollow.

'Interfering old bag. I'm *fat* compared to Victoria.'

'You're so lucky Carmen, your mother let's you do what you *want*.'

Paisley's moaning because her mum has grounded her until after Christmas. We're walking down to her house after school through the backstreets of Moseley, smoking fags.

Paisley has decided she wants to be friends with me now Maxine has been moved to a church school over in Edgbaston where they have to wear shit-brown uniforms and hats.

'Serves her right,' Paisley says, linking her arm through mine. 'Silly slag.'

Paisley's Mum is a social worker. She looks tired and harassed. Her hair is tied off her face with a scrunchy and she wears big hoop earrings. I like her. Her kitchen is warm and messy, with ashtrays, ketchup bottles, mugs and papers all over the table. The house smells of cooking and pot-pourri plug-ins.

'So who are you then?' she says, finally turning to look

at me. 'You're a pale one, aren't you? Want a bit of pizza?'

She opens the door of the biggest freezer I have ever seen. Inside it's like the supermarket: shelves full of Findus Crispy Pancakes, Birds Eye Potato Waffles, Sara Lee Chocolate Gateaux, Granny's Yorkshire Puds, McCain Oven Chips, Wall's Arctic Rolls, Captain's Cod Pies, McVitie's Cheesecakes.

'Mu-*um*,' Paisley says, bouncing on her seat, 'I'm sick of pizza.'

'Oi you, no moaning. You'll get what God puts on the table.'

Paisley rolls her eyes. 'But you're *not* God, Mum.'

'No, just close to it. C'mon, *choose* something, Paisley. I'm getting chilblains standing here.'

Paisley's bathroom looks different. They've put a new shower curtain up, and there's a rug over the cigarette burns in the floorboards.

Crispy pancakes and chips swim on the surface of the toilet bowl. I have to flush three times before they go away.

'You all right, Carmen?' Paisley asks when I come into her bedroom. She's putting up another poster. A boyband ensemble shines down from the wall. 'Doncha think they're sexy?'

''S all right,' I shrug.

She looks taken aback. 'Doncha like them?'

I shake my head, looking at her slyly. 'I like the Buzzcocks,' I say.

I play with Paisley's Barbies, bending them so that

Roller Skating Barbie and Girl About Town Barbie are in the sixty-nine position.

'Look,' I say, 'it's Maxine.'

There's a shop on the Stratford Road, just down from Nana's house – *Mighty Q We Sell Everything*. Arranged across the pavement there are plastic buckets of scourers, mops, dishcloths, sponges, dustpans, brushes, teatowels. Lava lamps bubble in the window along with china dogs and knick-knacks. There's a golden apple that Nana might like for her collection. A pair of mugs catch my eye.

*Best Mum in the World*, it says on one. *Best Dad in the World* on the other. Cartoons next to the curly red lettering: Mum is surrounded by ironing and washing up, Dad by cars and golf clubs and fishing rods.

I buy them both as Christmas presents for my mum and dad.

# 28

I have to let her in, she's got that many bags. Six, no seven, all full of food. 'Just a bit of Christmas shopping, love.' She can hardly carry them.

Mince pies, puddings, a turkey, packets of crisps, tubs of nuts, sausages, bacon, eggs, mayonnaise. All the trimmings. The fridge isn't big enough for it all, and she has to leave the turkey out on the side with a cloth over it.

She won't let me eat any of it. She says it's for Christmas.

'Hands off, piggy,' she says, when I pick up a barrel of honeyed nuts to read the calories.

She sits in the lounge reading aloud from Delia Smith. Step-by-step instructions on cooking Christmas Dinner. I concentrate on putting a new repair coat on my thumb. It's strange having food in the house again, like there's a visitor in the kitchen. A presence, which you just might catch if you open your eyes quick enough.

'I thought we were having dinner at Nana's.'

'We are,' she says. 'But it's Christmas, got to have food in, haven't you?'

We have a ready meal for supper. Marks and Spencer's best, though it still tastes grim. I only eat half of mine.

Mum doesn't touch hers. She sinks her fork into it and

leaves it on the arm of the chair. She looks at it from time to time, her eyes flicking away from the telly.

'I'm not really hungry,' she says eventually, getting up and taking our trays into the kitchen to scrape them into the bin.

Food fills my head. I can't stop thinking about it. All the things she's bought. I won't eat any of it. I *won't*. I'll be thin and beautiful.

I look at magazines. In *Mizz* there's flashy tight-fitting clubwear. Silver trousers and black T-shirts with *Punk* and *Rocker* in glittery script. *I want to look like that*, I think.

But when I check myself in the mirror, I look pasty, fleshy, stupid. My hair is growing back in silly tufts. I'll never be beautiful. *Never*.

I lie on my bed and chew my fingernails. Deliberately scraping off the polish with my teeth.

When she's asleep I sneak downstairs and take a few bags of crisps, a tube of peanuts. I tell myself that I'll save them for emergencies, but once I get them back to my room I eat them all, like I can't stop.

On the way back a peanut catches in my throat, making me choke. Mum knocks on the wall.

'You all right in there, Carmen?'

I flick my hands under the taps. As long as I can get rid of it I'll be all right. As long as nothing sticks.

In the morning, she checks all the cupboards.

'Where's the crisps?'

I shrug, refusing to look at her. She laughs.

'Couldn't resist it, could you, piggy?' She seems relieved rather than cross.

'Don't call me that!'

203

'Call you what I like,' she says. 'You're my daughter.'

She leaves for work. 'I've counted all the food,' she warns. 'I know what's there.'

I start on Lisa's Christmas present: a special set of nails. I've decided on a seaside theme and I've cut out stencils for a starfish, a seahorse, a fish, a jellyfish and, for the thumbnail, a hermit crab with a tall, conical shell and big claws.

She rings from work at lunchtime to tell me I can have a couple of slices of bread and a bag of crisps if I like. In the background I can hear the noise of the shop, the till beeping, dance music thumping.

''S all right, I'm not hungry,' I say.


We sit watching TV till eight, then nine o' clock. In the advert breaks she talks about what we could have for tea. Shepherd's pie, chicken curry, chips, sausage hotpot. 'Hotpot,' she says, 'I loved that when I was a kid.'

'We could have a banquet,' I say. 'We could have islands made of chocolate ice cream and lakes of toffee sauce.'

Mum smiles. 'Like queens.'

Neither of us makes a move towards the kitchen.


It's late when she says she's going for a drink with Victoria. Like nearly eleven. She doesn't even call a taxi or put any make-up on.

'I'll see you in a bit,' she says, wrapping herself up in her coat and slamming the door behind her.

When the doorbell rings a few minutes later, I think it must be her, realized that she'd forgotten her make-up.

It's Dad. I don't know what to say.

He stares at me really hard. I suppose I must look

204

different with my hair shorter and everything. 'Hello, love,' he says, rubbing my shoulders. 'Can I come in?'

Outside, it's started snowing, big sticky flakes that melt as they touch the ground.

'Hot enough in here. Your mother not in?'

'She's gone out.' I stare at him. He is smoother, healthier than he was before. Tanned and wearing a smart winter coat.

He stands in the lounge looking at everything. 'You been all right then?' he asks, studying the Dali print. 'That picture gives me the creeps.'

I show him the nails that I've done for Lisa. 'I haven't finished them yet.'

He smiles. 'You're good,' he says, simply.


He's bought me a PlayStation for Christmas. We sit down on the carpet in front of the telly while he plugs it in, just like he used to. We play *Wipeout III* but I'm not any good at it. I keep crashing into the sides and timing out. Dad wins every race.

'Out of practice, huh?'

He says he can't stop too long. That this is a flying visit. 'Where's your mother? She said she'd be here. We've got things to discuss.' He pats his briefcase.

He stares at me until I start to feel uncomfortable. 'Have you had any tea?' he asks.

When I shrug, he goes into the kitchen. I stand in the doorway, watch him opening the fridge. I want to tell him to stop being nosy. The food is ours, mine and Mum's. He fingers the unbroken plastic seal on the mayonnaise. 'How about a quick fry-up?'

He gets the bacon and eggs out of the fridge, heats some marg in the pan. I sit up on the kitchen unit and watch him. He asks if Mum is OK and when I say yes, he says that Mum can get sick even when she seems to be fine.

'You need to watch out for your mother's tricks,' he says. 'You don't have to follow her diets, you know.'

I kick my heel against the cupboard. I wish he'd go away. He's being patronizing.

'You don't know *anything* about her,' I say.

'That so?' He tenses, puts a rasher of bacon into the fat.

'Yeah.'

He piles food on my plate like he's taking the piss. Bacon, eggs, sausages, bread, tomatoes.

'Eat,' he says, tucking into his. I watch him shovelling it in greedily, chewing quickly, swallowing in lumps. 'Come on.'

'I'm not hungry,' I say, scraping everything, still steaming, into the bin.

He puts his coat on after that, seems in a hurry to leave. 'You tell your mother to ring me,' he says. 'ASAP.'

When he's gone I realize I've forgotten to give him his present. *Best Dad in the World.* I don't know why I bought it for him now. He's not even my real dad. I bury the box, all neatly wrapped and decorated with ribbons and bows, under all the food in the bin.

Ten minutes later there's the scratch of a key in the door. She's huddled into her coat, shivering. The snow has turned to rain, and she's soaked through.

'Mu-*um*. Where have you been?'

She says that she didn't go to meet Victoria at all, that she lied, that she hid in the phone box up the road. 'Thought he was never going to go.'

She sits on the sofa, and rubs her hands together. Her skin is blue. 'I can't face him, Carmen.' Her voice is far away, desolate. 'I'm a coward.'

# 29

We go over there about midday. Mum wants me to put on my Pocahontas frock, but I won't. She's only wearing a baggy jumper, and jeans made to stay up with a belt. I spend ages in the mirror putting kohl under my eyes and brushing my hair flat.

'Are you trying to make yourself look a mess?' she says, when she sees me.

It doesn't feel like Christmas really, except that the streets are quiet and all the shops are shut. We haven't opened any presents yet.

The hedge sprawls on to the pavement, it's getting thicker, small shoots sprouting from the base, growing greedily outwards and upwards towards the light.

Nana's in the kitchen, getting the dinner ready. Grandad's down the pub. We're going to join him later, 'just for a nip, while the dinner cooks.'

The tree in the lounge is a bit crap, just propped up against the side of the TV and not much bigger. Nana's threaded a bit of tinsel round it, but it still looks like no one's been bothered to make the effort. The telly's blaring and boxes of sweets and snacks are open on the coffee table: Mulberry Fruits, Quality Street, jars of fruit-and-nut mix, chocolate biscuits.

'What's with the tree?' Mum asks. 'Hacked it off the hedge, did you?'

'Your dad got it cheap, down the pub.'

We sit in the kitchen, watching Nana prepare the turkey.

'I hope it's defrosted properly,' Mum says, prodding it. Nana snips the string that binds its legs and pulls out a plastic bag of giblets.

'You'll have some, won't you, Maria?'

'Eugh,' is all Mum can say. 'Eugh.'

Nana rolls her sleeves up and pushes balls of stuffing up the turkey with her bare hand. It seems rude to look. I stare out the window at the dull green fronds of the hedge swaying backwards and forwards in the wind. When it's stuffed she pastes butter on the skin and lays bacon over the top.

Mum is tinkering with her cigarette, minutely examining the filter.

'Can I look now?' she asks. 'Is it in the oven yet?'

We're watching the Queen's speech when Lisa arrives. At first I don't notice, but when I look over my shoulder she's standing quietly in the corner staring at Mum. She's wearing a Dalmatian print jacket and her nails are redder than fire engines.

'Looks like Cruella's arrived,' Mum says.

Lisa ignores her, kisses me on the forehead and sits down.

'Happy Christmas,' she says to the room.

Nana makes us take our presents to the pub. 'You wait till you see what I've got Ray,' she says to us, beaming. 'I want him to open it in front of everyone.'

Whatever it is, it's heavy, and I have to carry the box all the way from the house to the pub. We go to the Firkin, a few streets away at the bottom of the hill. We have to go slow because Nana's knees are playing up. She leans on her stick and takes deep breaths, her buttery body shuddering with each step. Next to her, Mum seems like a doll. She's bent over like she's got something heavy on her back and, in the bright daylight, she looks older than Nana.

'Rocking Around the Christmas Tree' is playing on the jukebox and they've stuck scraps of tinsel round the ashtrays with sellotape. Mum laughs when she sees them.

'What's this?' she says, 'Christmas cheer?'

Grandad is at the bar, talking to a group of men who all look like him: same red faces, same nicotine-stained hair.

'Aye up,' he says, raising his eyebrows in a resigned kind of way. 'It's the women.'

'Get the drinks in, Ray,' Nana orders. 'Mine's an advocaat and lemonade.'

Mum orders Baileys for herself because 'it's Christmas' and a Diet Coke for me. When Grandad brings them over, Nana makes everyone raise their glasses.

'C'mon,' she says, nudging Mum, 'we're a family again.'

Mum and Lisa catch each other's eyes then look away quickly. Mum grabs my hand and squeezes it tight. Her fingers are nothing but bone.


'Open it, Ray, go on.'

Grandad looks at the box a bit taken aback.

'You shouldn't have, pet. We can't afford it.' He tears the paper off quickly like a kid. 'What's this then?'

'What it looks like.' *Black and Decker Hedge Trimmers* it says on the box. 'I got them off the shopping channel.'

Lisa breaks the silence by laughing. 'That's brilliant, Mum.'

'It'll take more than a pair of fancy scissors,' he growls.

'Oh, leave it, Dad,' Lisa says. 'It's Christmas.'

Mum cradles her Baileys, not really drinking it, only bringing it to her lips so it wets them with a milky film.

I get to give out my presents next. Nana is pleased with her golden apple. 'To add to the collection. Clever girl.'

Mum laughs when she gets her mug. 'It's *vile*. But so sweet,' she adds quickly. 'Look,' she shows Lisa and Nana, *'Best Mum in the World.'*

When Lisa opens her nails she smiles warmly, steadily. 'Did you do these? They're *gorgeous*.' And I know that she means it.

'Let have a look.' Mum leans over. 'Oh, Carmen, you should have told me you didn't have any money. You didn't have to make presents.'

I get a Walkman from Mum, a nail-painting kit and a book from Lisa and a big box of chocolates from Nana. The book is brilliant, full of design ideas and step-by-step instructions.

Grandad hasn't got anything for anyone, he says he's buying all the drinks.

'I put twenty quid behind the bar.'

'Tight arse,' Lisa says. 'You're a miserable old git aren't you?'

Grandad chuckles and puts his arm round Nana, giving her a sloppy kiss on the cheek. 'Wouldn't have me any other way, would you, Joyce?' Nana makes a face, but she's laughing really.

211

'Don't you want your Walkman?' Mum hisses in my ear when Lisa goes to get more drinks.

'No. I mean, yes.'

'Well stop looking at that bloody book then. You're showing me up.'

Lisa brings back bags of crisps from the bar. She gives Mum a packet of prawn cocktail flavour. 'Dinner's not for ages,' she says, giving me the cheese and onion.

Mum reads the calories on the back out loud. 'One hundred and ninety.' Lisa flinches and opens her packet, crunching defiantly.

Mum opens her packet and puts her finger in. 'Don't like this flavour.'

'I'll have it,' I say. 'You can swap with me.'

She passes the packet to me. 'No, you eat them, Carmen, you're always saying you're hungry.'

When no one's looking I drop them under the table and hide them under my feet.

We leave the pub at three when they throw us out.

'I'm starving,' Grandad says, rubbing his hands. 'Best meal of the year, Christmas dinner.'

When we get in, he unfolds the fold-down table that is pushed up against the wall in the lounge. He sits at the head of the table so he's got the best view of the TV.

Mum won't eat any turkey. She says the meat is too pink, that it's not cooked properly. 'Salmonella,' she announces, pointing to a pink streak in the thigh, 'is everywhere.' She puts a few sprouts and carrots on her plate.

'Not in my kitchen it isn't.' Nana sounds indignant.

'For *God's* sake, Maria,' Lisa hisses under her breath. 'You're putting us off our food.'

It's only afterwards that I see what I've eaten; when the potatoes come back nearly whole, the hard, crisped edges still visible along with the carrots and half-chewed pieces of sausage. I don't remember eating so much. It makes my nose run, my eyes go red round the edges. I use kohl eyeliner to cover it up.

Pig, I say to the mirror. *Pig.*

Lisa stares at me when I come back into the room but I won't meet her eye. She can't have heard anything. I let the tap run dead loud.

'You all right, Carmen? Have you been sick?'

'Of course she hasn't,' Mum says, before I can answer.

There is a pause that seems to suck all of the air out of the room. Lisa digs her nails into her palms. 'I can't *stand* it any more,' she says then, looking at Nana. '*Someone's* got to say something.'

Mum mashes her untouched vegetables into a tiny splash of gravy.

Nana and Lisa both stare at Mum.

'I'm worried, Maria. Brian's been to see me. He says you wouldn't meet him. All this dieting, this food thing, it's got to stop. You're sick, Maria. You need to get help.'

Mum smiles slowly. 'Just because *you've* let yourself go to seed.'

'Maria, love—' Nana says.

'Don't you start,' she warns. 'What do you know about anything? All you do all day is watch telly and eat. Always chewing like some bloody cow.'

Lisa frowns, runs her hands nervously through her hair. 'No need to be insulting, Maria.'

'It wasn't me who *started* it. Remember that. You can tell me the truth now, Lisa. After all this time I think I deserve that.'

213

'Don't be so paranoid, Maria. Anyway, I think there's a little secret we all know you haven't told someone. People in glasshouses and all that.'

All the colour drains out of Mum's face. 'You wouldn't *dare.*'

'Wouldn't I? Maybe I've had enough of covering up for you, Maria. Maybe I think you're messing up people's lives.'

'Girls, come on,' Nana says, 'It's Christmas Day.'

'I don't understand,' I say. 'What are you on about?'

No one will look at me.

Lisa bites her lip, a single fat tear rolls down her cheek. 'For Carmen,' she says, 'but not for you.' She nods at Mum, gathering up the plates. 'I'll get on with the washing up,' she says quietly.

'Lisa love,' Grandad looks up from the TV, his eyes pale, bleary. 'Any of those roast potatoes left?'

# 30

I'm getting better at *Wipeout III*. Mum stands behind me watching.

'Play it with the sound down, sweetheart.'

I do two perfect laps, only crashing on the third, and make it in time to move on to the next level. She complained about Lisa all the way home. 'You know, when we were younger, she was always on a diet. I don't know why she's having a go at *me*.'

She goes into the kitchen. I can hear rustling, cupboards being opened and shut. I don't pay any attention, do the next level in a perfect round of three. It's easier with the sound down somehow, less distracting.

Then there's the smell of bread burning. Plates clanking, toast popping. But then there's another noise. A small, muffled, animal noise. It goes on and on. A *lug*, *lug*, *lug*, like a snake swallowing an egg, punctuated by the rustle of cellophane packets.

I burn out of the game. I've lost my line, my concentration's shot. I don't want to move. I don't want to go into the kitchen. I don't want to see what she's doing.

She's in there for ages. I keep restarting the game, crashing a few seconds in, quitting and starting again, like my brain is in a loop.

When she emerges, her eyes are glazed; there are

crumbs on her cheeks, her clothes. I catch her out of the corner of my eye, trying to sneak up the stairs.

'There's food in the kitchen,' she says. 'If you want it.'

She goes upstairs, two at a time. She's running the tap, but I can still hear the retching. I turn the sound up on the game, start again from scratch, this time concentrating on keeping true to the line.

The turkey's still there. I think it's starting to go bad under its tea towel but everything else has gone. There are empty mince pie packets on the floor, biscuit wrappers in the sink, the jar of mayonnaise has been scraped empty, the loaf of bread is a crust, the nuts all gone.

I tidy up, put the wrappers in the bin. The box of Paxo is empty and she's even eaten all the margarine.

The toilet flushes and the tap goes off with a squeak. She opens the door to the bathroom and pads across the corridor to the bedroom.

When I go past her room I stop for a moment and listen. I can't hear anything. I don't know what I'm listening for. Breathing perhaps, or the mousy, murmuring sounds she makes when she's crying.

'You all right?' I knock on her door.

There's a muffled, 'Go away'. Then, 'Yes, I'm fine. Don't you worry about me, I'll see you in the morning.'

The house is starting to smell rotten. Mum says it's the turkey. That the central heating will have activated the bacteria. She wraps it in a bin bag and puts it outside. 'For the rats.'

She gets me to phone Theresa on her mobile. Half past nine on Boxing Day morning and Theresa sounds sleepy and pissed off.

'Mum can't come in today,' I say, biting my lip. 'She's sick.'

Mum watches, her skin is shiny with face cream.

'She'll manage,' she says, when I tell her that Theresa moaned. 'It' s what assistants are for. Anyway, it's not like there's customers. She's only got to get the sale stock out and price it up.'

Then she announces that she's taking the rest of the week off. To get her diet back on track. 'Starting with today.'

'Out there,' she says, waving her arms at the windows. 'It's all out there. If we stay in here we'll be fine.'

She checks the window locks, unlocking, then locking them again. 'I don't want it getting in.' She double locks the front door.

I ignore her and play PlayStation. She's turned the heating up and the air is thick and soupy with cigarette smoke. She's chain-smoking. After a few hours the need for fresh air is overwhelming.

'Can't we just have the window open a little bit?' I ask.

'No,' she says. 'I won't have it getting in.'

'Nothing's getting in, Mum.'

'Yes it is. All that greasy steam from chip shops, all the chocolate from Bournville. There's calories in the *air*, you know.'


She sits on the sofa in her bathrobe, sipping black tea, reading her diet books. She's writing out a New Year regime for us from a detox book. You're not supposed to do that programme for more than a few weeks because it's so extreme. It suggests a fast on the first day and Mum says that because we're pretty toxified from living in the city we should fast for a week. 'And then we can eat from their plan.'

I listen to her while I run lap after lap on *Wipeout*. I don't want to look at her. It was easier when there was food in the house. At least I could ignore it, pretend it wasn't there. Now there's this sicky, desperate feeling in my stomach, because I know that the kitchen is empty.

When she's done with writing her programme she folds the paper and stands it on top of the TV. 'So you don't forget.'

Up close, her ankles are bony and veiny, the skin transparent, like membrane.

The phone rings.

'Don't answer it,' she says. 'Leave it.'

It rings off, then rings back again. Mum unplugs it from the wall. She treads on it until the plastic casing cracks. 'I'm off duty.'

I'm starving but I don't want to tell her. I reckon the sooner I get thin, the sooner she'll get more food in, and when she goes upstairs to have a bath I get on the exercise bike. It's hot and I have to take my sweater off. I close my eyes and imagine that I'm in *Wipeout*. I'm zooming around the racetrack as I peddle, faster and faster, zipping around all the sharp corners until the wheels starts to squeak and my heart pounds.

I'm dizzy when I stop, and have to lie on the sofa, my lungs hurting. I can hear the thud of blood in my ears, the grind of the central heating, the hum of the fridge in the kitchen. It's like I'm waiting for everything to explode.

I dream about her. She's dancing, she's happy, the same as the photograph that Lisa keeps in the salon, turning around and around, her arms outstretched. She's got her eyes closed, she's concentrating, she's humming to herself. She gets faster and faster until I can't see her feet moving and she's spinning, a tornado of air gathering around her. The humming is echoing, deafening.

*Thinnnnnnnnnn*, she hums, *thinnnnnnnnnn*.

I wake up suddenly and I can't breathe. I don't know how long I've been asleep. The heating's still on, recycling the air, turning it stale. I go to open my window but it's locked. I push against the handle uselessly and try to control the panic that makes my heart beat faster. Outside the building site is closed up for Christmas, tarpaulins over the bricks, the roof joists. The house opposite is nearly finished and sold already. Mum said it was a young couple. 'In management. Our kind of people.'

We sit on the sofa together. I put my arms around her. She's freezing cold. She babbles on and on about food. She says that it's a curse, that women must endure it. 'It's sent to test us,' she says. 'But we're strong. We'll win.' She says we should imagine the house like a cocoon, that when we emerge we'll be thin, beautiful, powerful butterflies.

She dozes off about midday and I switch the central heating off, pushing all the buttons until the boiler stops humming. I try to open the front door but it's locked. I wonder if I should ring someone.

I look in all the cupboards. There has to be *something* to eat. But there's nothing apart from tea and coffee and Candarel. I dip my finger in the jar, lick off the sweet, chemical flakes. My hand shakes when I try to fill the kettle. I drink two glasses of water just to put something in my stomach. I feel crazy, hyperactive, high.

I wake her up with tea. She looks around her, dazed.

'Where are we?'

'I want to go out,' I say. I hold her hand, rub it between my palms, trying to warm it up.

'You'll run away from me.'

I tell her that I think we should eat something. Just a little something. 'I'm starving, Mum.'

'I *told* you. We're detoxing.' Her eyelids flutter. 'This is just a hard bit. We'll get through this, we *will*.' She grits her teeth when she says this, her face scrunched up, veins sticking out on her temples. 'We *will*.'

She goes to bed at six. She says we can eat something tomorrow. 'Five more days, honey, only five more days.'

When she's upstairs I look for the keys. I can't find them in her handbag or her coat pockets. She must have taken them upstairs.

She's padding around her bedroom, talking to herself. I plug the phone in and try to dial Lisa's number but the keypad's not working. It makes a funny beeping noise when I punch in the numbers. I try Nana. Same thing.

I bang on her door. 'Let me in!' I scream, desperate. 'Let me in!' There's rustling inside. 'I'll break it down.' I press against the door with my shoulder. '*Mu-um*. Let me in.'

When she opens the door, she's holding a key in her hand. 'Go on then,' she says, her lips a half-smile, mocking. 'You can go if you like. Miss Piggy off to trough.'

I snatch the key out of her hand. 'I'm sick of it,' I hear myself shout. 'You're not fat. You're *not*.'

'Sweetheart,' she says, 'you don't understand, I don't *deserve* to eat.'

Something in my head erupts. Mad kaleidoscope colours swim in front of my eyes. I breathe lungfuls of the sharp night air. I try to focus. All around our house are building materials: huge sewer pipes, piles of bricks and timber, A-frames for the roofs, bags of concrete. A piece of loose tarpaulin flaps in the breeze, making me start. I hug my arms to my chest, start running out on to the main road. I let my feet carry me, racing along the pavements, my body light and brittle as a bird.

# 31

*Boxing Week Beanfeast* it says on the banner outside. *Mexican Madness.* The car park is full, cars glistening in the evening frost. I'm steaming like a racehorse and swaying on my feet. When I close my eyes to catch my breath I open them again quickly, scared that I'm going to pass out.

The restaurant is packed and dingy. There are hosts at the door, women dressed in stripy, toothpaste-green uniforms, pillbox hats pinned at jaunty angles to their heads. People are queuing along the servery, filling their plates from the trays of food. The salad bar looks like the aftermath of a food fight, the vats of coleslaw and potato salad spilling into oily pats on the floor.

I can't see Billy. Dickie's behind the bar, pulling pints. When he sees me, he comes over and grabs my arm. 'What happened to you?'

'Billy,' I gasp, 'I want Billy.'

'He's in the kitchen.' He points to the swing doors at the back of the room.

I can't see him. The kitchen is dazzling, the light reflecting off the chrome surfaces almost blinding. The air is full of steam and grease and noise. There are baskets of chips boiling in the fryers, chickens turning on the rotisserie, griddles of burgers spitting, waiting to be flipped, pizzas crisping in the ovens, steaks hissing under giant salamander grills, flames licking over the meat-like tongues.

Two boys in stained overalls rush between the ovens and the counter, shovelling chips into big metal trays, dolloping ladles of gloopy cheese sauce on to steaks, emptying portions of stir fry into woks, fire leaping up as the fat spills over the edges.

'What d'you want?' one of them shouts over the roaring of the air conditioning. He wipes a smudge from a plate with a blackened cloth.

'Billy.'

He points behind him with his thumb. 'Out back.'

I squeeze past them to get to the door. The floor is slippery and I have to slide my feet to stop myself falling over. They both stand still for a second to let me pass and I see that they're both soaking: their chefs' whites stained and singed and wet with sweat. They smile, their faces red, broiling, overheated.

Billy's in the store cupboard wiping his jacket with a bit of blue roll. He's got a greasy stain down his jacket.

'Some kid throwing food about,' he says. 'You come over with your mum?'

When I shake my head he stops wiping.

He tells me to keep an eye out for the cops because he's over the limit. It's miles back to the house. I've no idea how I found the way here. 'Did you walk all the way?' Billy asks.

'No, I ran,' I say simply.

He sucks his teeth. 'Young people.'

The house is silent when we get in. She's not in the lounge or the kitchen; all the lights are off.

'Maria!' Billy calls up the stairs. No answer.

He takes them two at a time, opens the door to her bedroom. He takes a deep breath when he switches on the light. 'Oh God,' he groans.

I look over his shoulder. She's not there. On the bed her fake Louis Vuitton cases are flung open. Inside them and scattered all over the bed, the floor, are wrappers. Old pizza crusts, KitKat wrappers, foil from ginger cakes, boxes and boxes of Ferrero Rocher chocolates. She must have been stashing it for months.

She's in the bathroom. The door's locked and there is a hiss of a tap running. Billy bangs on the door.

'Maria! *Maria!* Are you all right?' No answer. He turns the handle, pushes against the door. 'I'm going to have to break it down,' he shouts.

Suddenly, the door flies open, but it's not my mother who stands in front of us.

She stares, her eyes wild, sunken. She's wearing her long nightdress, the pink one, and it's come open over her chest, except there's no chest there any more just bones pressing through the skin like weals. Behind her, the bath is spattered and blocked with brown sick.

She slips through the gap between us like a ghost, screaming that she wants to be left alone. She runs out into the street and off up the road. Billy dials 999 on his mobile.

When they catch up with her, she's half a mile away, nearly in Northfield. The ambulance almost knocks her over, and for a second, before the ambulance men over-power her, wrap her in blankets and administer a sedative, she's like a figure from the painting: spectral in the head-lights.

They make us wait in the corridor. Billy gets some teas from the machine. 'I got you this as well,' he says, giving me a Mars Bar. I put it in my pocket for later.

The doctors put her on a heart monitor, slide a glucose drip in her arm. They tell us that she's starving. That her body has been eating away at itself for months, that now she's started to digest her vital organs, the muscles around the heart, the lungs.

Billy looks upset when the doctor says these things. 'We've never known,' he says, 'how to stop her.'

He grabs my hand and squeezes it. We sit there for a moment in the Family Room, hand in hand.

'I'm sorry,' he says, quietly.

# 32

Nana's out the front in her mac and a pair of wellies. She's leaning on her stick with one hand and wielding the trimmers at the hedge with the other. Greenery falls down around her like rain.

It takes ages to cut through the dense growth to the trunk of each bush and then lop the top off.

*'Timber!'* she cries, as another one falls into the road.

We watch her for a few minutes, then Billy goes into the house and switches the trimmers off at the plug.

'*Ray,*' she squawks. 'I told you I won't be doing with it any more.'

When she turns round, she puts the trimmers down and hobbles towards us. 'If it's about your mother I don't want to hear it.'

The kitchen is lighter already, bright shafts of winter sunlight flood in. 'I *knew* that this would happen when you came back. I *knew* it.'

She won't go to the hospital. She tells Billy to fetch Lisa first.

I finger the Mars Bar in my pocket. I still haven't eaten anything and, for once, Nana hasn't got any food out. She's staring out of the window. She clears her throat a few times.

'I've never been much good at talking about these things, pet.'

I unwrap the Mars Bar, push it between my lips. The sweet, sugary chocolate melts on my tongue. I savour it for a second, then eat it, nearly whole.

'What could I do? Worried me sick when she came back. I could see what was going on but it's always the same, she never listens. It's like drugs. She can't help herself.' She turns from the window to look at me. 'I won't have you going the same way.'

'I won't,' I say, swallowing a hiccup.

She turns back to the window. 'You know, I've forgotten what it's like to have a view.'

They put her on pills. They give her all kinds of trial combinations. Green ones for her mind, yellow ones for the side effects, blue ones to make her hungry. She keeps pulling the drip out of her arm. Worried doctors write notes about her weight. Six stone three. Same as prisoners in Belsen in the war. Every day the nurses put her on the scales and weigh her to make sure she's gaining.

She shields her eyes from us when we come in. 'Go away,' she says. 'I don't want you to see me like this. They're trying to make me fat.'

Afterwards Nana and Lisa talk to the doctors in a private room with glass mesh on the windows. They want to move her to the psychiatric hospital in Winson Green.

We're waiting for a bus outside the hospital when I decide to leg it. I'm sure they've been talking about Social Services and foster homes behind my back.

I get lost trying to find town, end up by the canals in Brindley Place. There's loads of posh cafés, people in business suits slipping discreetly in and out of bars. Some of them have even got seats outside. I sit in front of the windows of Café Rouge until I get so cold I have to move.

I know where I am when I find the Library and Paradise Forum. I buy a juice from Starbucks with the last of my money. I don't know where I'm going to go.

Walking down New Street all the women look like dolls. *Robots!* I want to shout at them. You're all robots!

I start to swing my arms, left, right, left, right, higher and more rigid each time. People are starting to stare. 'You all walk like this!' I shout at them. '*Robots!* You're all robots!'

When I get to the bottom of New Street, everything's a mess, the city is rubble for nearly half a mile. I stand against the mesh barriers, looking down to where the markets used to be, the Nail File. They've blown up nearly the whole Bull Ring, only St Martin's church still stands forlornly in the middle.

Lisa taps me on the shoulder.

'Thought I might find you here.' She must have been following me.

I shrug away. 'What do *you* want?'

'Come on, Carmen, love, your nan is worried sick.'

'Wants to put me in care more like.'

I light a fag, won't look at her 'No one ever said that,' she says.

'No, just *thought* it.'

She gives me a don't-be-silly look. 'I've got a proposition for you.' She twists her fingers through the mesh and smiles. 'Come home with me.'

I've been here before. I recognize the kitchen. The bright yellow units, the blue-check curtains.

We stopped off at Sainsbury's on the way home. Lisa's got big bags of shopping. She says we're going to do some cooking. 'I'm going to show you how to make a proper shepherd's pie.'

She lays everything out on the kitchen table, explaining how you have to sauté the onions first, and then add the veg and the mince. She tells me how to make the potato creamy by adding butter and milk to the mash. She gives me a peeler. 'Here, you can start on the potatoes.'

We work together in silence for a while. I feel suddenly awkward, like I'm getting in the way.

'I'm sorry,' I say.

'What for?' Lisa looks at me sharply. 'Don't you start getting paranoid on me. You belong here, we're you're family. Don't you forget that.'

When we've put the potatoes on a low heat to boil, Lisa unknots a bag of onions. 'There's one bastard thing about being me that I hate,' she says, eventually.

'What?'

'I always have to be the one who says the things that no one else wants to say.'

'Like what?'

She sighs. 'It's about time you knew,' she begins, 'about Billy.'

I know what's coming next, like I've known since I met him, like I've known all my life, even though I've never even thought it until now.

'He's my dad,' I say. 'Isn't he?'

Lisa wipes onion tears from her cheeks. 'Who told you?'

I shrug.

'You mum should have told you. I expect she was trying to. I think that's why she brought you back here. Oh, Carmen, I'm sorry.'

My head is spinning, though outwardly I'm calm. I try to comfort Lisa, tell her it's OK. But it's like the ground under my feet is tilting, turning to sand.

'I got the fright of my life when you cut your hair,' she says. 'You're the spitting image.'

She sits down, cleaning her fingers on her apron.

'After you were born your mother got very depressed. Not like I'd ever seen her before. She'd give you to Billy to look after and then lock herself in her room at Nana's and not come out for days. Billy was a bit different then to how he is now, you know, he was still a bit – well, unreliable. He used to bring you round here to stay with me. I looked after you for nearly a whole year while your mother was sorting herself out.'

She pauses and looks at her hands, idly picking at a chipped nail.

'And then when she got better and she met Brian she just whisked you off to Yorkshire. She went really funny on us, she said that me and Billy were trying to steal you away from her and that as far as she was concerned, you didn't have a father. She got it into her head that I was having an affair with Billy. Ha! Me and Billy. Chance would have been a fine thing.'

The potatoes rise to a boil, spilling white foam over the sides of the pan. Lisa reaches out to turn the heat down. 'I've, er, invited him round later. I hope you don't mind.'

The kitchen is full of warm steam. Outside there are powder-puff clouds in the sky, curtains furling like flags in the breeze.

'No,' I say, eventually. 'I don't mind.'

Paisley's redecorating. She's taken all her posters down, the shiny faces of Westlife and Boyzone and 5ive are crumpled in the bin.

'I'm not a kid any more,' she announces, putting her Barbies in a big shoebox.

She got a new stereo for Christmas and we're listening to *Never Mind The Bollocks* at top volume. 'Mum and Dad hate this shit,' she says proudly. 'They're *hippies*, godsake.'

I tell her about Billy, about Mum.

'Man,' she says, rolling her eyes, 'that's so, like, messed *up.*'

She's bought a new set of make-up in dark reds and silver. She shows me her new lipstick, a thick black with glitter in it.

You like it?' she asks. 'Try it on.'

I wipe it across my lips, all the while watching myself in the mirror. It makes me look mean.

''S wicked,' I say.

'You can have it then,' she says, grinning at me. 'I wish I had my hair done like you.'

'Got any scissors?' I ask.

She looks at me doubtfully. 'D'you think that's a good idea?'

'Oh, not for you,' I say, picking one of her Barbies out of the box.

We start by stripping them. I rip Ballet Barbie's tutu as I pull it off. When they're naked, still pouting inanely, we cut off their hair, until a tumbleweed of flaxen locks lies on the dressing table.

'They're so *stupid.*' Paisley says, drawing zigzags on her Barbie scalp with eyeliner.

'Let's burn them,' I say.

We go outside, round the back of Paisley's house, into her garden. The security light flicks on, flooding the garden with a brilliant white light. There's a concrete barbecue at the bottom, past the fishpond and the crazy paving. We huddle around it.

'Shall we dismember them first?'

'No,' I say, decisive. 'They deserve to be burned *alive.*'

We lay them on their hair, side by side, arms reaching stiffly upwards. I set fire to the bed of hair with a lighter, and flames leap up with a whoosh.

The dolls curl and melt, their plastic shells shrivelling into their hollow bodies. They give off an acrid chemical smoke that makes us cough. When the fire dies down, it leaves a hissing mass of molten goo that sticks to the barbecue as it cools.

'Wow,' Paisley says, poking it with a stick. 'That was so, like, *radical.*'

There are faint traces left in the blackening ooze: fingertips, toes, even a nose and a mouth, a single blue eye. I shiver, not because I'm cold, but because I can feel my skin tightening, like cling wrap pulling taut, around the soft contours of my body.